D0661837

Tavish

A Time Travel Romance

JANE STAIN

Copyright © 2016 Jane Stain (Cherise Kelley)
All rights reserved.
ISBN-13: 978-1541141360
ISBN-10: 1541141369

The Renaissance Faire Series:
Renaissance Faire
Renaissance Festival
Renaissance Man

The Dunskey Castle Series:
Tavish
Seumas (2017)
Tomas (2017)

The Hadrian's Wall Series:
(2017)

And more to come!
Sign up for new book alerts at

janestain.com

DEDICATION

To Scott. I love you.

Contents

ACKNOWLEDGMENTS

Thank you for beta reading, Jimmye and Vicky. I owe you each a big favor.

Thank you, Omniglot, for posting online the Scottish Gaelic numbers from one to a hundred. I enjoyed numbering my chapters with them.

Thanks to a Scottish pilot who prefers to remain anonymous, we have the lovely photograph of Dunskey Castle on the cover of this book, and a video and many more photographs on the Facebook page for the mother of all my book series:

https://www.facebook.com/RenaissanceFaireKilts/

Aon

Kelsey examined a beaten silver necklace, holding her phone close so Sasha could see. "Yes, this interlace pattern is at least a thousand years old, probably older, judging by these animal designs woven in along here. Sec, let me zoom in. See?"

"Wow. It does look like it. Have you done the chem bath yet?"

"No, I'm just about to. Here, you can watch."

Kelsey could barely contain her excitement, even as her nose stung from the acrid smell of the chemical tests that would give the necklace's age within a hundred years. Her foot bounced impatiently while she let the university's automatic computerized microscope do its thing and she admired her surroundings outside the canvas flap door of the work tent.

The ruined tower house sat on one of Scotland's high craggy sea cliffs, with a view over the ocean of the distant green hills of Ireland. The fifteenth century stone house called Dunskey Castle had been built over the ruins of a much older fortification, rumored to be an underground palace chipped out of the very rock, with secret passageways right down to the sea. Her grey-haired client had recently won a court battle to come into ownership of it all, after his family had all but abandoned it five hundred years ago.

Even as much as the work excited her, she itched to get done so the client could take her on the tour he had promised. He had flown her all the way from the U.S. to examine some artifacts he had found in chests in one of the three previously sealed and secret cellars.

Well, now she would tell him he had a trove of antiques—and he would give her a big payment!

Her eyes drifted back to her laptop, and she paused them there, analyzing what she saw and searching for an explanation. Her training kicked in, telling her to collaborate with the trained colleague that protocol had caused her to invite along, if only by phone.

"Are you sure you can't come by, Sasha? This necklace is odd. The patterns aren't matching up with any in the computer. It's still searching, but it's going slower and slower."

Sasha's redheaded face appeared in the corner of Kelsey's screen.

"No, I have to lecture this afternoon, sorry. But tomorrow's the weekend, maybe then. I just logged in so I could see. Fascinating. Maybe you'll catalogue an entire newfound strain of Celtic expression."

"Wouldn't that be something?"

Kelsey wanted to say more, but the boyfriend she had loved and lost came bustling into the work tent, completely distracting her. And not only because he was bare chested.

Bronze haired and brown eyed like Kelsey, Tavish MacGregor had been a nosy construction worker at every last one of her Scottish clients' ruins these three months—after completely dropping out of her life seven years ago. No contact for seven years, no explanation, he was acting like nothing was wrong, and he always stubbornly wore that red and green plaid great kilt that made him so darn sexy she could just...

Oh no.

Kelsey sat up straight and smiled at her client, whom Tavish seemed to be dragging in on the hem of his kilt.

"I have to go, Sasha."

"Business?"

"Yeah, call you back tonight."

Typical. Tavish had wandered away from his own work and was looking at hers.

"'Tis na 'Celtic jewelry,'" he said to Mr. Blair. "Nay, it be not auld warld."

And he said this in his sexy accent that had drawn her to him in the first place. Not to mention those twinkling brown eyes that could see into her soul whenever they wanted. And those strong arms that had made her feel so loved and cherished, all those years ago. And his fighting prowess that had protected her a time or two...

Kelsey blinked herself back into the present and turned to her client, to gauge his reaction to what Tavish had told him.

Mr. Blair looked skeptical, but patient.

"Hold on, nae. Let the doctor finish her appraisal, lad."

Ha, Lad. Good thing someone was around who could put Tavish in his place. She didn't trust herself to try—and besides, she was a professional woman now, not the teen she'd been when she and Tavish had been together.

She gave her client a patient conspiratorial smile, which he returned. This made her feel warm inside. He respected her expertise, unlike some people.

With the young virile man and the grey stooped man both watching, she finished her complicated high-tech tests on the necklace. Unwilling to believe what she saw and trying not to scowl, she tested a silver goblet next, and then an ornate bronze breastplate.

Finally, she had to admit that Tavish was right.

The items weren't old world at all.

How did the kilted fool know this stuff better than she did? He hadn't even gone to college, let alone researched a doctoral thesis on the meanings of ancient Celtic runes— like she and Sasha had.

"I'm sad to say Tavish is right, Mr. Blair. This is indeed imitation Celtic art from the twentieth century. It's well done and will probably bring five thousand pounds from fans of historical cosplay, but not the hundreds of thousands the Royal Museums would have given you for true antiques. I'm sorry."

Mr. Blair gave her a sad smile and his digital signature for her usual fee, not the huge bonus she had heard you could get from an overjoyed patron who had struck it big. As he handed her phone back to her and headed out of the tent, his eyes fell reverently on the ring Kelsey wore on her right hand.

Her ring from Celtic University.

Crafted in the same style as the items she appraised—and oddly shaped—this silver ring represented seven years of study in a highly niche discipline at the most prestigious university in that discipline—which only awarded three doctoral degrees every five years.

And she held one of them.

Had for three months now.

And Tavish had… what? That stupid kilt he wore all the time? His stupid Scots accent—which by the way he could drop anytime he wanted to and speak like a normal American? No, she knew exactly what he had.

"You've got some nerve, Tavish."

He raised an eyebrow.

"What nae?"

"Who do you think you are, coming in here and butting in on my business?"

As soon as she said it, she knew she sounded childish and wanted to take the words back, but it was too late for that, so she rocked back on one of her legs and crossed her arms, figuring she might as well entrench her position.

Infuriatingly, Tavish puffed out his chest, crossed his own arms, and gave her that smugly coy look which used to always make her kiss the smugness off of him.

"Yer business? I hae the duty of seeing this place restored correctly."

Ooh. He had so much nerve, she was going to—

But Tavish nodded to himself, and his gesture took in all of her equipment as well as the trinkets she was examining.

"It is ye, lass, who are in the way."

Seeing red, she closed her eyes so she wouldn't have to

look at him and opened her mouth to tell him how rude he was being, how Mr. Blair himself had invited her here, and wasn't it up to the landowner to say who needed to be on his property or not?

But when she opened her eyes again, Tavish was halfway through the tent flap already. Once more, he'd just waltzed in on her doing business and made her look foolish. Had made what she did look so easy that even an uneducated construction worker could do it. She had to tell him he couldn't do that to her. She wouldn't take it.

But not in front of the client. Not where he could hear her. She looked around for Mr. Blair and found him on his phone out of earshot, outside. She could see him walking along the cliffs by the sea in the sunshine that had just broken through a small hole in the roiling Scottish storm clouds.

She turned to Tavish's disappearing form and yelled after the flapping hem of his kilt.

"It's not like I planted those trinkets in the man's basement for him to find, you know."

And then she blew her nose to hide the tears in her eyes, in case someone came into the tent. While she stowed her handkerchief in the pocket of her blazer, she admired the soft light gray wool of her skirted suit, proud of how professional it was. She remembered fondly how her mother had tailor-made it and five more just for her— dark gray, dark brown, camel, navy blue, and olive green. She cheered herself up by recalling how much fun the two of them had, shopping for matching blouses and shoes. Professional, but still feminine and pretty.

How on Earth did Tavish know so much about Scottish artifacts? Why did he have to always show off like this whenever she was in Scotland? It was like he made it a point to be there, just to make her look bad.

Apparently, their relationship had meant more to her than it had to him.

Obviously.

Taking a deep breath and blinking her eyes while fanning them with her hands in order to dry them without smearing her makeup, she tried to look on the bright side.

Her career was solid outside of Scotland, away from Tavish. She had proven her parents wrong. They hadn't taken it well when she told them what major she was declaring—which was ironic, seeing how they were the ones who had gotten her involved with the Renaissance faire when she was little.

The faire had interested her in all things Celtic.

And the faire had introduced her to Tavish.

And then she'd chosen to major in Celtic Studies way back in her freshman year at college because of all the Celtic fun she and Tavish had made for themselves at the faire.

She fought to maintain her composure so as not to look a fool in front of her client when he came back into the tent, but she was getting lost in a sea of memories, triggered by his presence.

For her first few months at Celtic University, she had texted Tavish whenever something cool or unexpected happened. Had emailed him photos of her dorm room. Had kept calling him and leaving messages.

But then someone else had answered and told her she had the wrong number.

The same thing had happened when she called his parents.

Finally, she had taken the hint, given up, and thrown herself into her studies.

And now after seven years he had shown up at her job sites three times in three months—apparently just to make her clients doubt her abilities. Why? Why couldn't he just stay out of her life completely?

She smoothed imaginary wrinkles out of her skirt. She needed to have a word with him. In private. No one needed to know their business, least of all her client. But how—

Oh good, it looked like Mr. Blair was preparing to leave. Yep.

He came back into the tent and picked up his briefcase, then shook her hand and gave her a grateful smile.

"Doctor Ferguson, it's an honor to be doing business with you. It's a shame about those… supposed artifacts, but we have found a passageway to the sea through the old cellars. I yet hold out hope that we will find the underground Alba castle. If we find anything at all, I'll be calling you back here to help us look into it. You can count on that."

She gave him as firm a handshake as she could manage, and she returned his warm smile.

Mr. Blair turned his head toward where Tavish could be seen talking and laughing with the other construction workers and then turned back to her with a knowing look.

"Please tak yer time packing up all yer things, Doctor, and enjoy a look aroond if ye like. I've been called into toon for the rest o the afternoon."

She stood up and opened her mouth to tell him it was okay, she would leave when he did.

But the elderly gentleman closed his eyes and gently

shook his head no while holding up his hand and also waving no.

"There's a washroom that functions ower thare in my trailer, which is unlocked. Please sleep there this evening if it gets tae dark tae drive back into town. Nay trouble at all, and help yourself tae any o the canned food. The men all hae their own trailers up the road."

This was just too much kindness. It made a tear escape and slide down her cheek. She brushed it away with the back of her index finger.

"Thank you so much, Mr. Blair. I may take you up on that offer. Thank you for the opportunity to see your lands and all that has come with them, and have a safe trip into town."

Mr. Blair nodded toward the outside.

Kelsey grabbed her purse and got up to follow him out.

She saw him to his car and waved as he drove off, and then she ran to his trailer to get ahold of herself.

It was tough at first, because this trailer reminded her of Tavish's family trailer at the faire, where among other things she had giggled over pancakes on Saturday and Sunday mornings with them.

She was really glad to have her purse and a functioning washroom. She washed her face and reapplied her makeup, then went back into the work tent by the castle to repack her equipment, glad to have something simple and easy to do while she figured out what to say to Tavish when she caught up to him.

Because she was going to ask him what the hell he was up to. And tell him to quit it. To either be nice, or leave her alone and stay out of her business.

But Tavish was already there when she got back to her

stuff. And he had already repacked it for her. Her stuff. Her expensive professional instruments that he had no idea how to use or probably even what they were for.

Her mind whorled and a torrent of insults came to the tip of her tongue. But she bit it. She was a dignified professional appraiser, not some shrew who shrieked at a construction worker. Not where anyone could hear her.

"Well thank you, Tavish, for cleaning up. Now I have time to see the rest of the estate before it gets dark. Do you want to show me around?"

Good. This was a surprise to him, and he looked a little off balance. But it was just for a moment, and then he recovered.

"Okay. Yeah. I'll just carry this stuff out to your car first so you'll be all ready to go, and then I'll give you a quick tour."

Why was he in such a hurry to get her out of here? Oh well. Let him think it would be a quick tour and then she'd be leaving.

"Thanks. If you can get those two heavy ones, I can get these other two."

The svelte muscles in his arms moved in fascinating ways as he scooped up her two heavy equipment boxes in no time at all and then stood off to the side to let her pass.

Darn. He still had manners.

"After you," he said.

"Thanks."

As she led him out to her rental car, she used her pretty gray high-heeled shoe to kick some loose stones out of the way—and was satisfied to see them fly.

Why was she thanking him as if *he* would be the one staying in the owner's trailer tonight? She was the senior level contractor on site, the one with the most training and the biggest credentials. How did he manage to always be in charge?

She opened her trunk, and he packed her equipment away. She stowed her high heels, got out her boots and socks, sat down in the passenger seat, and was putting them on over her pantyhose when Tavish came right up to her and decided to make small talk.

"Oh, good. I was afraid you were going to break your ankle on our little tour, in those impractical shoes."

So that was how they were going to play it, huh? Act nonchalant. She took a deep breath and then came up with a genuine smile at the prospect of the tour.

"No way. I came prepared to find out just exactly how extensive the secret passageways are."

At the mention of secret passageways, a little of the young Tavish, her Tavish, came back in the twinkle of his eyes.

"You wouldn't believe how extensive!"

They grinned at each other for a moment, just like old times.

But then his smile fell.

"Oh, but you don't have time even to go down one of the secret passageways."

Her face must have looked puzzled, because he gave her a pitying look.

"You really don't wanna be driving back to town after it gets dark. There aren't any streetlights, and the roads twist and turn every which way."

She decided it was time to set him straight about just how much time she was going to be here with him.

"It's okay. Mr. Blair gave me the use of his trailer." She

looked up at where the sun could barely be seen through the thick Scottish clouds. "We have at least 4 hours of daylight left. Even I can hike down to the water and back in that amount of time."

He gave her the thinnest of smiles, but then he put his hands on his hips and turned toward the castle.

Preparing for him to tell her she had to leave, she sat up straighter in her rental car. If it came down to it, she would call Mr. Blair and have him tell Tavish what was what.

But that giddy smile came back on Tavish's face.

"Do you have a heavier coat along? Because it can get pretty cold down there, even in September."

Smiling, she grabbed her parka and leather daypack out of the back seat.

Dhà

The tower house was mostly just three stories of crumbling stone walls. It was large, about a hundred feet by fifty feet, but had no roof. The true attraction was the rumored underground castle inside the cliffs the house sat upon.

Kelsey pointed to where the castle yard dropped off the cliffs into the sea and started walking over there quickly, doing her best to be the dignified appraiser and not show too much excitement.

"Let's go down into the caves."

Tavish fell in step beside her and gave her a wistful smile.

"We haven't found the way into most of them, but we have been able to get down to the sea through one, and there was that room with the trinkets you examined today." He stopped suddenly and grabbed her hand, lending calm support just when she felt herself tripping. "Watch your step. The foundation of an older structure sticks up just enough to trip over, like right there."

A thrill went through her at the touch of his hand. She held onto it for a moment, in order to catch her balance as she looked down and saw the half-inch which remained of a stone wall, sticking up out of the grass, and then she let go as casually as she could, still tingling from his touch.

"Thanks, I think I will watch my step."

He smiled with just a pleasant amount of teasing and started walking again.

"Good idea."

She followed his flapping kilt through a tour of the teetering tower house. It had a surprisingly open floor plan for a structure that was a few hundred years old. It must have been a party house. She didn't think she would have enjoyed living in it. She preferred a network of small rooms with doors she could close so that she would have quiet to read while people in the other rooms visited or sang or played games and did other loud things.

Ooh, just as she had suspected, there was a cellar in each of the three smaller rooms on the ground floor.

With a ceremonial flourish, Tavish pulled up a modern plastic covering to reveal the first dark hole in the ground.

"When the estate came into Mr. Blair's hands, these three cellars were hidden. The only reason we found them was because of the rumors of their existence. It took quite a lot of experimentation with fancy acoustic equipment that could detect hollow areas underground."

Kelsey could see where this first cellar had been opened with brute force by the construction workers. It didn't have stairs, but Tavish and his crew had installed modern metal ladders, which looked really odd against the stone. Without being asked, he let her go down first, in her skirt. Knowing he had nothing on underneath his kilt, she made herself look away and resisted fanning herself as he came down the ladder next. Everything interesting had already been taken out of the cellar, of course, but exploring was fun. The cellars were irregular, and carved out of the rock cliff.

She and Tavish had climbed out of the second of these three cellars when they heard dogs snarling nearby.

The sound made Kelsey's knees weak, and she leaned against the outer stone wall of the castle. She didn't realize Tavish had run off until she turned to where he had been a moment ago and heard him yelling from the nearby bushes.

"Ha! Ha! Git! Ha!"

She then heard a dog crying and another one barking, and she yelled out to Tavish.

"Are you okay?"

"Yeah. I'll be back in a minute, soon as Tuffy runs off. Go on, Tuffy! Go home! Go home!"

Kelsey's feet were running over there before she knew it. She rounded the corner and saw something she never would have believed if she hadn't seen it with her own eyes.

Tavish was holding a largish dog in his arms almost like a baby, except he had its legs trapped off to his sides and he was hugging it close so that its snarling mouth couldn't get to his throat. His face was all business, with no hint of fear for himself.

On the ground, a smaller dog was barking at the largish

dog while running around in circles and jumping up as if he could attack the bigger dog.

Tavish was talking to the smaller dog, visibly concerned about its welfare.

"Go home, Tuffy!"

Kelsey gasped. Her voice sounded really high when it came out.

"Did you grab that dog while it was snarling at the other one? Are you okay? Did it bite you?"

He turned so that he could see her behind the dog he was hugging.

"Yeah, I'm fine. Will you take Tuffy back where the guys can protect him, Kel?"

She laughed at the little dog, who was still maneuvering around to try and get to the larger dog somehow, he thought he was so tough. She kneeled down.

"Okay, yeah. I will if I can catch him. Come here, Tuffy!"

The little dog ran right into her arms, and she laughed her way back toward the work tent, at how he never stopped telling the bigger dog off or trying to get to him.

One of the construction workers saw her coming and cupped his hands around his mouth, calling out behind him, "Gus, the woman's got your dog."

Gus turned out to be a huge older guy. He held out his arms as soon as he saw his dog, and Kelsey had to bite her tongue to keep from laughing at how he spoke to his pet.

"There ye are, Tuffy wuffy. Why'd ye hae ta go and run away, eh?" Once he had the dog in his arms, he raised his head up and spoke to her while petting Tuffy.

"I thank ye, lass, from the bottom of my heart. If ever there be aught I can do for ye, let me know right quick, ye ken?"

She'd observed Gus in the group of construction workers with Tavish earlier, good-naturedly laughing and talking with him. Her gut told her she could trust this old highlander, and that he was capable. She smiled at Gus and lingered for a moment to speak with him about how Tavish treated her.

"Well, there is one thing you can do for me…"

When she got back to Tavish, she felt a little guilty for taking so long, because he was still holding the bigger dog. He didn't look any worse for wear though, and his only concern seemed to be for the little dog.

"Is Tuffy safe?"

"Yeah. Gus has him."

Tavish let the bigger dog go, and it ran off past the ruins into some bushes.

She ran her eyes up and down Tavish. His previously bare chest and arms were covered with a linen shirt and a plaid woolen cloak now, but his hands and face were still bare. There wasn't a scratch nor a mark on any of it.

But just as she relaxed in the knowledge that he hadn't been harmed, a weird feeling of unfamiliarity took hold of her. Now that she looked at him in the sunlight that peeked through the clouds, he looked about five years older than her. Wrinkles were forming around his eyes and mouth. Not smile lines, either.

"Wow, Tav. Construction work must have you out in the sun a lot, huh?"

Ignoring her question, he just smiled and rushed back toward the third cellar, calling to her over his shoulder.

"Come on!"

Once they were down inside this last cellar—which was

more elaborately lined with stonework and had clearly been used as a root cellar—Kelsey saw the secret door right away. It was in the corner, clearly labeled with intricate lacy Celtic runes carved into the stone. She went over to get a better look.

Tavish frowned at her oddly.

"Yeah," he said, "that's right where the secret doorway is, to the sea passage. How did you know?"

Oh, so the man did *not* know everything after all. Feeling a little guilty about how much that pleased her, she refrained from gloating when she pointed out the runes. They were gorgeous, and their style suggested they were at least a thousand years old, maybe even two thousand.

"These right here give it away."

He wrinkled his brow at her in a question.

"They're like a door sign that says 'Passage to the sea.'"

Good. He looked impressed. He raised his brows then and turned to look at them and follow one of the curlicues with his finger.

"Do they tell you how to open it? Because it took four of us a good month to figure that out, after it taking another month just for us to notice it."

She looked all around the old stone portal. Yep. There were arrows carved into the pattern, and a kind of series of movements...

Stone against stone made for a really odd sliding sound, but once she had the correct direction—at a weird angle indicated by the arrows—the section of stone in front of her slid a few feet easily with her push, revealing a dark passageway that opened to her right, bringing with it a cold breeze that made her shiver a little and zip up her parka.

She turned to Tavish with a triumphant smile.

He gave her a congratulatory one in return, and they stood there grinning at each other for a moment as if they were fifteen again, about to sneak off on another adventure away from their parents.

On the verge of going into the darkness with Tavish, it occurred to her there might be a very logical reason for him to basically ignore her whenever he saw her—when he wasn't finding fault with her, anyway. On impulse, she asked about it.

"Tavish?"

"Yeah?"

"I only see a ring on your right hand, but um, that doesn't mean anything for guys these days. Um, are you married?"

And there he was again, the old Tavish. His eyes got that twinkle in them. It was an amused look, but not one that was laughing at her. He was laughing with her as they used to do, laughing at the strange but wonderful circumstances they found themselves in.

"No. No, I'm still single."

On hearing this, a dizzy dancing feeling filled her. It started at her heart and radiated out to her extremities—and she grew warm. Her body was telling her to grab him and kissed him and hold tight to him and never let go.

But just in time, her brain served up a memory of how rude he'd been not an hour ago. She took a deep breath and let it out audibly, blocking those irrational desires from her mind.

But the fact that he was single was good news. There wouldn't be some wife getting upset if rumors started about the two of them being alone down here. That would be terrible for business, especially if it made it into the paper or something. Yeah, it was really good news. For that reason.

No time at all had passed. Tavish was just now getting over the laugh they had shared.

She was liking this lighter mood.

"Oh," was all she said before turning into the passage and opening up her leather daypack to rummage around for her flashlight.

He took his own flashlight out of a loop on his construction-worker's utility belt, and they were ready to go.

"After you," he said again, gesturing gallantly but with a sincere look on his face. "Later, it gets a little rough, but right at first here you don't need to watch your step yet."

She wasn't going to argue. She took him up on his offer and rushed through the doorway, for once not worrying about how eager she looked or how it would let him know this was her first big adventure as a professional Celtic ruins appraiser.

"Thanks."

She was impressed at first that it didn't smell musty down here, but she remembered that the passageways opened up to the sea. And then she shined her flashlight down the cave and gasped.

Down here, the walls were carved out of solid stone. Ancient carvings. But it wasn't ugly at all. It was wondrous. This wasn't a cave. It was an underground palace.

After every few feet she walked, she couldn't help looking over at Tavish and pointing out to him how smooth the stone was, how gracefully the ceiling arched, how beautiful the Celtic interlace carvings were that graced the walls here and there.

He smiled back at her and nodded each time, and then she went back to exploring.

They came to a three-way fork, and Tavish indicated the right branch.

"Down that way is the dead end we think has hidden doorways to the underground castle. Do you want to go down there and check it out, or go to the left down toward the sea?"

"You know me," she reminded him. "Which way would I find more interesting?"

He pointedly looked at her Celtic University ring.

"I'm not really sure I *do* know you well anymore, but the Kelsey I remember, the adventurous one, she would have insisted on checking out the passage down to the secret doors."

"I'll make you a deal," she said to him.

Wow. He gave her a soft look that she never thought she'd see again. It made her want to hug him…

"I'm listening," he said.

Right. They were just talking. What was she saying, again? Oh yeah. The deal.

"I'll be the Kelsey you remember, if you'll be the Tavish I remember."

Oops. What had made her say that?

The soft look left his eyes, replaced by wariness.

"You know what—" he started.

But she cut him off.

"Not for always, Tavish, just for this tour of the passageways, okay?"

He sighed heavily, and sadness filled his face while his posture relaxed as if he'd been ready for a big something and then just given up.

"Okay, but Kelsey, when this tour is done, promise me you'll go into Mr. Blair's trailer and stay in there until the sun comes up. Please, promise me."

Taken aback by just how desperately worried for her he seemed, she agreed to his terms without any negotiation.

"I promise."

He visibly relaxed.

"Thanks, Kelsey."

And then his eyes were looking far away, and he started to reach out to her, and then let his hands drop.

She stomped her foot to get his attention, to make him look her in the eye. Okay, and maybe she was trying to get him to laugh a little, too. She'd always found foot stomping ridiculous.

"What's wrong, Tavish?"

But it didn't work. He looked away.

"I can't tell you."

Now it was she who relaxed her posture and sighed heavily and kind of gave up.

"So that's how it's going to be?"

For a moment, his eyes met hers and his mouth opened and he was standing up straight again, and she thought he would say no. That he would change back into the Tavish she had known and loved. The one she knew had loved her. But it didn't last. She saw the exact moment when he closed down and shut her out.

"Yeah, that's how it has to be."

Tears tried to come again, but she marched on down the right corridor, put on her professional demeanor, and let the wonder of the old stonework push aside her hurt feelings.

She'd come to see the ruins, not Tavish.

And these worn underground stone hallways were amazing. The Celts had obviously occupied this site before 'civilized' people had built the stone tower house up above—no, much longer ago than that. Even before whoever it was had built the older structure up above, the one that was just a half-inch of stone above the grass now.

She rushed on ahead of Tavish, following a path the interlace carvings promised would lead to a storage room. Dimly aware of him following her but no longer pointing out her discoveries to him, she pushed through two more secret doors and went down a narrow cut-stone stairway.

Trì

Tavish trailed his hand along the rough stone wall to slow himself as he followed Kelsey down the narrow stone staircase.

On the one hand, he had to get her out of here. They had expressly told him to keep her away from the ruins at night. They were ruthlessly territorial, and despite what a court had said about this being Mr. Blair's property, they claimed first dibs on any artifacts. They were always looking for certain ones, and now was no different. He'd been told to keep his eye out for one item in particular.

On the other hand, it was a few hours until sunset, and whoa. He and the crew had spent months digging out this first passageway, and then Kelsey wanders in and finds another two secret doors after just a few hours? Part of him didn't want to stop her until she'd discovered all the other secret entrances hidden in these ruins. This second part of him was winning, so far. He would just quietly follow her, observe—and make sure she didn't do anything that would make them too mad.

Kelsey had reached the bottom of the stairs and was inside a small room that had been cut out of the natural rock, gazing all around with wide eyes.

"Oh, look at this place."

When he caught up to her and leaned into the tiny room, he saw what made her marvel so.

"I expected everything to be covered in dust," he told her, taking in all the odd shapes in the room almost as much as the pretty sight of her.

"I did too," she said without looking away from all the items carefully stored here, "but look how advanced the ancient architecture is." She pointed while she spoke. "See how these tiny windows are cut precisely opposite one another?"

"I wondered where the wind was coming from." He nudged away from the wall with his shoulder and leaned forward slightly, toward where she was pointing.

"Come stand here," she said, impatiently gesturing for him to join her in the middle.

He balked, because it was really close quarters.

She reached out and grabbed his arm and pulled him in, as if he were a disobedient child.

He felt himself smiling despite his need to keep her safe from them—which meant uninvolved with him—and he fought to make his face serious.

"There," she said, "now don't you feel the wind hitting you from all sides?"

Mostly, he just felt the bottom of her long soft skirt rubbing against his bare calves and the tug of his kilt against the front of him, where it had caught against her parka. But he couldn't say that.

He concentrated on making his voice businesslike.

"So you think the wind is clearing the dust away?"

"Yep," she said. "Cool, huh?"

"Not as cool as how you just waltzed right down here as if someone had drawn you a map. How did you know where those secret doors were, let alone how to open them?"

That did it. Kelsey finally looked him in the eye. She was scowling, but it didn't ruin her pretty features. And then she rolled her eyes, held up her hand with the Celtic University ring on it, and pointed at the ring with her other hand.

His throat was suddenly dry, and he swallowed. Other than that, he just stood there waiting for her to answer him. It was weird, seeing this mature businesswoman in front of him, wearing a suit and speaking of architecture. In his mind, Kelsey was still the one friend he'd had in his teen years, the only one who kept in touch with him between the times his parents' traveling Renaissance faire came to her town.

Of course he was glad she'd grown up, but seeing her cultivated mannerisms always caught him off balance. Well, if he was honest with himself, then he would have to admit that what bothered him was how much more educated she was than him. He felt intimidated by her, and his manliness didn't know what to do with that feeling, let alone the envy he felt. She had attended school like a normal child, while he and his twin brother and their two cousins had taken lame online classes, with no one to hang out with between weekends except the kids of the few other traveling Renaissance faire workers.

She tilted her head to the side, crossed her arms, and stood there waiting in return. Maybe she was even tapping her foot, but he didn't dare look. If she was, that would make him laugh, and he knew she wouldn't appreciate that right now.

Gradually, it dawned on him, what she wanted him to say.

"Okay. I guess there is something to your doctorate degree."

She sighed.

"About time you realized that."

But then she turned and looked at the room again, then back at him. She grinned from ear to ear, and her whole body jiggled a little bit. She pulled two fists toward her with a sudden jerky movement.

"Yes! Look what we found! It was so fun Tav, studying for real all the stuff you and I could only dabble in at the faire."

Pride in her accomplishment surged through him, and he did his best to show it in his smile.

"It shows on your face whenever you talk about it. I'm glad you've found work you love, Kel."

At the word 'work', the smile left her face and she started to meticulously check all of the artifacts and garments and tools in the room. He didn't know what she was checking them for, but she sure seemed to know what she was doing.

And this was Kelsey.

Her prim tailored suit, warm parka, and hiking boots covered most of her, but he was still transfixed by the way she moved and by how absorbed she was in what she was doing. And then she started digging in her bag, and he knew she was after her phone. To take pictures.

He held the wrist of her hand that was digging in the bag.

"Kelsey."

She tried to pull her wrist away.

"I have to document this, Tavish."

"I can't let you do that, Kelsey."

"What?"

"I just—"

"You know what?" She was huffing, and the two of them struggled, both of them talking at the same time.

"I know you really want to take pictures of this stuff, Kelsey, but you can't just go—"

"Tavish, I'm not just some stupid girl who wants to take pictures of this stuff—"

"—barging into places you don't know are safe and—"

"—I'm an appraiser who Mr. Blair hired to go over anything discovered here—"

Oh yeah, Mr. Blair.

Tavish eased off his hold on her wrists, and she pulled away, caught herself before she fell against a large standing figurine, and took what must have been her professional lecturing stance, because she started lecturing him.

"—and taking pictures of how artifacts are found is part of the process. I need to post them to Celtic University's site to document the way they were stored. It might give us insight into Celtic beliefs and technology. I don't expect a construction foreman to understand, but I do expect him to show me the professional courtesy of getting out of my way."

"Kel, I'll get out of your way, but you need to call Mr. Blair and get his permission before you post any of those pictures online. Can we agree on that much? This is his property. He has rights."

She took a deep breath as if to argue with him, but then let it out and kind of deflated.

"Yeah, you're right."

She dug some more and finally got out her phone.

"Kel, that's not gonna work down here."

But she held it up for him to see, pointing at three bars.

"Wanna bet?"

Huh. That was one extensive set of windows down here. They weren't letting any light in, just wind, so how were they letting the phone work? Oh well, it was working.

She put her phone to her ear. A huge grin broke out on her face just before she started speaking.

"Mr. Blair? It's Dr. Ferguson. I am so sorry I got your voice mail. Guess what. Tavish and I found an entrance to the underground castle!"

Tavish smiled back at her when her eyes found his, and he pointed at her and nodded and then pointed at himself and shook his head no.

She wrinkled her forehead at him and held her hand out to the side, as if to say, "I give you credit and then you don't want it? What's wrong with you?"

He whirled his finger around in a circle to indicate all the stuff in the room and then pointed at the phone.

She nodded quickly.

"We're down in it right now, and you won't believe

how much stuff, I mean how many artifacts, are preserved just in this one small room. I'm taking pictures to document the find in its pristine condition. We won't disturb anything until you give us the okay, but I'm itching to post these photos to Celtic University's password-protected site so that my colleagues can see them. Please call me back about that as soon as you can. Thank you so much for letting me look around without you here, but I am so sorry we actually found this in your absence. I'll stay here tonight in your trailer, and hopefully you can come by in the morning. I'm so eager to show you this. Bye for now."

She hung up and proceeded to take her pictures.

Good, she wouldn't disturb anything, and that would have to do. He hoped it would be enough to pacify them. But as usual, they wanted him to find something for them here at this site. This room seemed as likely a place for it to be found as any, so he came back into the room with her and joined in her examination.

He asked her what he knew must be annoying questions, but he needed to keep her engaged so that she didn't do anything he'd regret.

"What are all these little tools for?"

She didn't get annoyed, though, just answered as a teacher would, reveling in sharing knowledge.

"I'm pretty sure they're to carve designs into the stonework."

"Like the designs you showed me in the root cellar?"

"Yeah, just like that. They're all over the tunnels. That's how I found my way down here."

He looked at the old iron tools neatly lined up in their case, wondering why they hadn't rusted away.

"So with these tools, you could make some more of those designs?"

A look of wonder came onto her face, and she stooped to look at the tools longingly.

"Yeah, I think I could. They wouldn't be as good as the ones that are already there, though, and of course they wouldn't be as old, so they wouldn't fool someone who knew what to look for."

"Someone like you?"

"Yeah!" she said with joy, "Someone like me."

He scanned the room for their precious item, throwing out comments as they occurred to him, to keep her from noticing.

"What's all of this white cloth over here?"

"Those are ceremonial druidic robes. The druids are the Celts' priests, you know."

"The druids are Celtic?"

"Yeah."

"No, I didn't know that."

She gave him a smug look and continued photographing everything. She kept her word to the client and didn't disturb anything, but she went over everything very closely, so he was 99% sure that what they wanted wasn't in this room. Well, you couldn't expect it to be that easy, or those who sent him wouldn't need him.

Every once in a while as the two of them looked at the stuff, they would brush against each other, and the old passion would threaten to flare up in him. Aw heck, it did more than threaten. He would need a cold shower tonight.

Finally, she was finished with the room and turned toward the doorway, lit up from head to toe with excitement.

"This room is great, but it's a dead-end. Let's go on back up the stairs and look closer at that old laundry room. I'm positive there are more secret passageways that go out of it."

"Naw," he said, looking at his own phone, "it'll be dark soon, and this area is full of wild animals like that dog you saw earlier. We really don't wanna be outside once it gets dark. And while it's really cool down here," he said, "the part we've found so far doesn't look very comfortable, and I doubt there's running water in any case, let alone flushing toilets."

She groaned.

"You're right. Okay, walk me back to Blair's trailer?"

"You got it."

They started up the stone staircase. He stayed behind her so that he would block her if she fell, but to his relief, she looked quite nimble.

"Tavish."

"Yeah?"

"When Mr. Blair comes tomorrow, let me take him up to that room."

"I'll let ya, but I'm coming with."

"No."

"No?" He tried to keep the amusement out of his voice when she turned around to look at him sternly.

"No."

He reached toward her at the same time as she started walking down toward him. He'd meant to tap her leg to get her attention so that she turned around, but now she was falling toward him.

Her breasts collided with his face.

That wasn't the worst of it though. Suddenly, he was

holding her in his arms. She felt so good there, just like old times. He cleared his throat and looked into her soft brown eyes with regret as he slowly steadied her on her feet again.

"Sorry. I just meant to stop you so we could talk."

"I know."

Darn it. He could see the old passion stirring within her, too. This was the last thing he'd meant to do, make her want him again. He couldn't be with her. She didn't know how dangerous that would be for her, and he couldn't tell her. He wished his parents had told him sooner, so that he hadn't let her get close to him in the first place.

Oh well. Done was done, but he wasn't going to let her get trapped in this life. Besides, she had changed. He didn't trust the professional appraiser she had become. She seemed like someone who would sell off the seven wonders of the world to the highest bidder, rather than make them museums for everyone to enjoy. She wasn't the Kelsey he used to know, and he needed to remember that.

He released her and took a step down, which was awkward because he was talking to her breasts, which were clearly outlined by her form-fitting parka. He did his best to look into her eyes.

"Kelsey, I know you think I'm just a construction worker, and officially, that is all I am. But I have a duty here to... to protect the Scottish national heritage. I have to be along with you wherever you go in Scotland."

She gave him a look of incredulity, and then she crossed her arms over her breasts—thank God.

"Wherever I go in Scotland? Like, even in the cities? You think there's ancient items of Scotland's national heritage in the cities, too? Oh, and then hadn't you better meet me at the airport next time I come to Scotland? We wouldn't want me to disturb any precious national heritage items in the terminals, now would we?"

He sighed.

"You know there aren't. You know I mean just out in the countryside, at castles and other ruins."

Her face cracked into the slightest grin.

"In other words, about ninety percent of the country."

Despite himself, he chuckled a little at that. At least she still knew how to have fun and wasn't always this stuck-up, hoity toity, 'doctor' person.

"Come on, Tavish. You aren't really out to protect the Scottish national heritage. What's this really about?"

"Like I said before, I can't tell you."

She sighed.

"So we're back to that, huh?"

"Afraid so."

"Really?"

"Yeah."

"I can walk myself to the trailer."

She stiffly turned around and marched up the stairs. He waited until she was five steps ahead and then followed her as quietly as he could.

There really were animals about. And worse.

Ceithir

Kelsey knew Tavish was following her, but she pretended not to notice. Let him be the ignored one for a while. Too bad she didn't have seven years to ignore him and not answer his calls or emails to even let him know she was alive. That would be payback.

She continued to ignore him even as she got to the door of the trailer, then went inside and set her backpack down and closed and locked the door behind her. If he wasn't going to be friends with her and tell her what was going on, then why should she talk to him at all? No reason, that was why.

So she took a quick shower, and then while she microwaved some canned ravioli, she called Sasha instead.

"Hi Kelsey. So are you away from Tavish and free to talk yet?"

"Yeah."

"Oh Kelsey. You let him get to you again, didn't you."

"Well he was different this time, Sasha."

"Not different enough, or you wouldn't sound so sad."

"True."

"You didn't—"

"No, of course not. I didn't even let him in the trailer, even though he followed me all the way back here right after telling me he couldn't explain what was going on."

"He was probably just being a gentleman, Kelsey. And I'm glad he was. You're basically in the wilderness out there and really shouldn't be outside alone after dark."

"You're probably right. I mean, about him being a gentleman. But it's so confusing. One second we're staring intently into each other's eyes and I'm sure he's gonna kiss me, and the next second he's not wanting to explain to me what's going on with him."

"Kelsey, if I've told you once, I've told you a thousand times: you can't go by what a man does. If you think a man cares about you and wants to be with you in a meaningful way, wait for him to actually say so."

"Uh... yeah. Well, now that we've gotten that over with, let's talk about you for a while."

"Ha! Fair enough. Well, it's time I admitted it: I envy you, getting to do field work. A professorship sounded so prestigious when I accepted the job, but you're on the verge of a real discovery there, I just know it."

"Oh Sasha, I'm so stupid. I should've told you right away."

"What?"

"We do have a find. Here, let me show you the pictures." She fiddled with the files in her phone, working to bring up the pictures she'd taken with Tavish earlier.

"Hurry up and tell me already, don't make me wait for

the pictures. I'm dying of curiosity."

"Here they are. I took tons, so I'm just gonna flip through them slowly and let you look. Stop me if you need to." She flipped through the pictures for several minutes, and all the while, Sasha ooh'd and ah'd. And then when they were done, her friend groaned.

"Oh, why did I take this professorship? All I do is lecture and read papers. Boring! I'm the wild and crazy one and you're the calm cool collected one. We should switch places."

"No way, but if you want, come on over tomorrow and check it out."

They talked for an hour, and then Kelsey fell into bed exhausted, but feeling a lot less alone and frustrated.

But Tavish was waiting for her in her dreams.

She dreamed of his parents' Renaissance faire, where she and Tavish used to dance folk dances together, run around the field in games of rounders and relay races—which was difficult in her long skirts and his kilt—act in plays, walk arm-in-arm in parades, and cuddle in his family's trailer while his parents were busy elsewhere.

Tavish had been so nice back then, the perfect boyfriend for four years, even though he didn't go to her high school and she only saw him during the summers. During the school year the two of them would text constantly.

So it had been all the more hurtful when he'd stopped responding to her texts that first fall she was at college.

Fast-forward to three months ago, when she'd gotten her first field assignment here in Scotland. There he'd been, acting like a stranger. And here he was now, not acting much better than a stranger. And sometimes it looked like he thought she was his enemy.

But in her dream, the two of them were snuggling in a trailer much like Mr. Blair's. They were seventeen again, but somehow they were talking about what had happened today, when they were twenty-five. Well, it was a dream…

Kelsey broke off their hot french kiss and sat up away from Tavish, giving him a serious face.

"What the heck is going on, Tavish?"

He looked confused.

"What do you mean?"

She mimicked him.

"What do you mean?"

He looked just a tiny bit annoyed, but mostly amused, and he gave her his best and sexiest smile.

"Come on, quit acting like a kid."

She pointed at her heart with her finger.

"Me act like a kid?"

He shrugged, apparently resigned to keep playing her game.

"Uh, yeah."

She took a deep breath and tried to be twenty-five, but she stayed seventeen. Darn this dream. She let the air out of her lungs and felt sort of deflated. But then she got an idea. She gave Tavish her sweetest smile and caressed his face the way that used to drive him crazy.

"You're the one who's keeping secrets."

Something weird was going on now though, even for a dream. She could see it in his eyes. He was twenty-five inside too, and he knew what she was talking about.

"Aw, come on Kel. I can't tell you."

She let the hurt show on her face, which was something she would never do with the real twenty-five-year-old Tavish. No way. She wasn't going to play the fool to someone who couldn't be bothered to tell her what was going on.

"You can't tell even me? It's me, Tavish. We used to tell each other everything, or at least I thought so. I told you everything. I kept on telling you everything for months, even when you never answered my texts or my emails."

And then, for just a moment, she saw pain in Tavish's face. Heart wrenching pain just like her own.

"They took my phone away, Kel. I…"

"You what?"

"You have to know I still love you."

"I still love you too, Tavish."

"So why are we fighting?"

"Because like I said, you're keeping secrets."

But then the moment was over. Twenty-five-year-old Tavish was gone. Her seventeen-year-old boyfriend was sitting in front of her again. The knowledge and the pain had left his face, and he just looked mystified.

"I'm not keeping any secrets from you, Kel."

"You're not?"

"Nope."

"Promise?"

"Promise."

The dream got private after that, and she really enjoyed it.

~*~

At the crack of dawn the next morning, she awoke with a pleasant sense that something had been resolved, but she also had this nagging feeling she'd found out something important, but couldn't remember what it was.

When she opened the trailer door, Scotland greeted her in all its glory. The pink sky cast its light over the fields of heather and the craggy mountains and the rocky shoreline so that for a moment all she could do was stand there and stare. Truly, only the ruins of an age-old castle could promise more delight, and it just so happened there was one right here. She took off running in her hiking boots.

She only got halfway to the third cellar's trap door before Tavish was with her. And of course he couldn't just wear jeans and a hoodie, like she was today.

"Do you always have to wear that kilt?"

Oh great. That was the wrong thing to say. He struck a pose, teasing her with it. He knew she thought he looked hot in a kilt.

"Aye lass. That I do."

She put as much annoyance in her voice as she could.

"Why? That has got to be the most impractical thing a construction worker could wear."

At first he was smiling, clearly enjoying her grudging admiration. But then a shadow of the pain she had seen in her dream crossed his face, and he relaxed out of his pose.

"Never mind. When is Mr. Blair getting here?"

She held up her phone.

"He hasn't called back yet, but I'll be ready when he does."

She started moving toward the root cellar again.

He fell into step beside her.

"So where are you going?"

"I don't need to have Mr. Blair with me to go check out the rest of those secret doors, Tavish."

"But—"

"But nothing. My client told me to go ahead and look

around at the rest of the property, and that's what I'm doing."

"Well I'm coming with you."

She made sure he could see her roll her eyes.

"I can see that."

"Kel—"

"Don't Kel me. That's a name my friends use."

There it was again. Pain showed in his face, and for a brief moment he looked at her pleadingly. And then that hardness came back into his eyes. He held out his hand toward the root cellar door rather formally.

"You're right, Dr. Ferguson. Please allow me to escort you."

"Fine. After you, Mr. MacGregor."

He let her open the secret door inside the root cellar. She blocked his view with her body and tried not to smile at how smug she felt, knowing that he probably didn't know how to do it her easy way. She went straight back to that old fashioned laundry room where Mr. Blair had found the trinkets, because she was sure she'd seen the outlines of a few more secret doors in there.

When she saw them, she forgot she wasn't talking to Tavish anymore, she was so excited.

"I knew it."

"There are more secret doors?"

"Yep, three of them."

He looked around, but it was obvious he had no idea where they were. He looked right past them. It was on the tip of her tongue to tell him what to look for, but then she remembered he wasn't her friend anymore.

This time she let the smugness show on her face.

"Here, the first one's this way."

"You know, Dr. Ferguson, when Mr. Blair gets here, he's not going to want to go down to the sea. Don't you think we should go down there and check it out now, before he gets here?"

He was right. How considerate.

She narrowed her eyes at him, mostly playfully. He knew darn well she wanted to go down to the sea. And of course this was something he could take the lead in, having been down there before.

"I suppose you're right, Mr. MacGregor." She graciously gestured toward the doorway, the same way he had gestured toward the root cellar door earlier. "Lead the way."

Her subtle attempt to regain control of the situation had not escaped him. He raised his chin and flounced as only a kilted man can flounce.

"I dinna mind if I do."

She forced herself into professional demeanor, stuffing her irritation. Unfortunately, she wasn't able to stuff her attraction toward him. Her only consolation was that he seemed to be having the same trouble, cold one moment and warm the next. Would he just make up his mind? Wait a minute, no. She'd already made up her mind. It was like Sasha said: don't pay attention to what a man does. Wait for him to actually say you mean something to him. Never assume you have his commitment, no matter what he does. Wait until he actually says he's yours.

The trip was worth the aggravation, though. The farther down they went, the less finished the passageway became, until they were walking through a natural rugged cave. She greatly enjoyed the contrast. She could tell they were almost down to the opening because of the freshness

54

of the air when she saw a large section of dozens of strange vertical grooves carved into the raw cave wall and stopped to ponder what they might be.

"Do you know what those are?" Tavish asked.

"No, but I get the distinct impression you're about to tell me."

She looked at him then, and he looked smug.

"They held bows, and quivers full of arrows, for guarding the docks down there."

Now that he said so, it made sense. She could see where the bows would go, and the quivers.

"How do you know all this, Tavish?"

He shrugged and then smiled at her over his shoulder, taking off at a run.

"Come on. The cave mouth's just a little farther."

She followed him, and then of course there was the Irish Sea.

Ireland herself greeted them from across the sea—far enough away that they couldn't make out any details, but close enough to be within reach, to make Kelsey curious what lay over there in those lush green hills.

Tavish sounded as excited here as she'd been up in the rock-hewn storage room full of artifacts.

"They've docked boats here in the past. See the tie spots?"

Sure enough, long ago someone had pounded crude iron rings into the cave wall near the water's edge next to natural stone docks where you could climb aboard a boat. The boat would be sheltered from the waves by the cave, but there wouldn't be far to go at all before you would be out at sea. You could probably motorboat over to Ireland in less than an hour.

Unable to help herself, she smiled up at him in pure delight.

"Don't you wish we had a boat now?"

"I really do. I've been trying to get Mr. Blair to bring one so he could, you know, check out his portion of the coastline—and maybe motor on over to Ireland."

They laughed.

"You mean so you could."

He nodded with a smile.

She looked over at Ireland, along the coastline, and then back at the tie spot.

"This is the most awesome dock I ever saw."

"I knew you'd like it."

She looked back across the water at the Irish shore where she could see two distinct cities complete with ports, one of them very large.

"Yeah, we need a boat here."

"We?"

"Yeah, we."

"Kel—"

"Mr. MacGregor, now that there is so much more to the estate, so many artifacts to document and catalog, my client will ask me to stay on for at least a month, probably three."

Tavish took in a deep breath like he was going to lecture her—but then he grabbed her hand and ran for the passageway up.

"Let go of me."

"They're coming, Kel."

"Huh?"

She looked over her shoulder and then tugged on his arm and dug her feet into crevices in the rock, trying to stop him from dragging her back up.

"Tavish, that's the most gorgeous old Celtic boat I could ever have imagined. Let me go."

"That's danger, Kel."

He grabbed her and threw her over his shoulder in a fireman's carry, and ran back up.

Unable to act on her anger and indignation, she let the professional part of her calmly note how odd the cave looked from the perspective of someone whose head was bobbing upside down. And in that frame of mind, she had a surprisingly calm discussion with the man who was manhandling her.

"Where are you taking me?"

"Back to the trailer."

"But I want to check out those other secret doors."

"Never mind those Kel, at least until Mr. Blair gets here."

"Mr. Blair doesn't seem the type who could protect me from the kind of danger that would make a MacGregor run."

At that, he chuckled the tiniest bit.

"It's complicated, Kel. Just trust me."

"It appears I have to."

"You'll be safe in the trailer, Kel."

But when they got to the old fashioned laundry room, they could both hear harsh voices coming down the corridor toward them from the root cellar.

"Her presence here is a problem."

"We'll deal with it."

"She'll distract him."

"He'll find it."

"He'd better."

"He will. He's one of our better workers."

She barely heard Tavish uncharacteristically swear while changing direction and going down the middle corridor, the one they had never discussed. How weird. She'd kind of forgotten all about that middle corridor.

But those voices. They were familiar. She couldn't quite place where she'd heard them before, but she knew she had. Her mind kept showing her images of who it might be, and she kept rejecting them, one by one, like watching an old movie and being sure you'd seen one of the actors in something before, but not knowing what…

He kept her in the fireman's carry hold the whole way down to where the middle corridor ended in a nondescript dead-end. And then the walls whirled and blurred in front of her eyes as if she were seeing them from the bottom of a whirlpool.

Còig

They wouldn't follow him and Kelsey to the old time. They never did go there with him, even though they were the ones who had given him the ring and shown him how to use it. She would be safe there—at least from them.

He would find what they wanted from this underground castle in the old time. It would pacify them. It had to.

There were so many things he wished he could grab before he took her to the old time, but he could tell by the sound of the approaching voices that he had less than a minute, and he needed to use as little of that time as possible.

He took Kelsey down the guarded hallway and turned the ring on his finger.

The blurring came. He'd learned that if he focused on one thing during the blurring, he was less likely to get dizzy from it. At least he knew there would be no one around when they arrived. He was always careful to time travel only when there was no one in the travel spot.

At last, the whirling stopped.

They were in the old time.

"Here, let me put you down," he said to her as he did so.

Kelsey spluttered and stumbled a bit when he turned her back over and set her down on her feet.

"Finally. I thought my head was going to pop, it was getting so full of blood. I bet I was just about to pass out. I was getting so dizzy, the walls looked like they were spinning around." She stood still for a second with a far-off look in her eyes. "Well, whoever was saying it was bad that I was in here must have left, because I don't hear them anymore. Who was that, Tavish? And what did they mean about you being one of their best workers?"

He sighed and gave her the most sincere bracing smile he could manage.

"Don't get mad, okay? Please don't raise your voice, and especially, don't go down the hall yet."

Her eyes went down to the opening of the hall and back to him.

"Tavish, you're kind of scaring me."

He looked in her nervous brown eyes and tried to

project concern and caring. And he took a giant step to put himself between her and the way out of the hallway.

She scrunched up her delicate brown eyebrows and narrowed her now angry brown eyes at him, then reached up to push him in the chest. She barely moved him.

"What are you doing? If this is some sort of game, it isn't any fun."

He took a deep breath and let it out, then walked about 10 feet up the hallway toward the opening, turning to encourage her to follow him and then waiting until she had caught up.

"Do you see anything different about the runes on the walls now, Kel?"

She blinked, turned to look where he pointed, briefly looked back at him again with a question in her eyes, and then turned to intently study the runes, running her finger along them and gasping every so often.

"Wow! I didn't even notice these when we came in. Of course, that's not too surprising, seeing how I was upside down and bobbing around. But wow. Judging by the relative lack of stone erosion, these runes are at least a five hundred years newer than all the others, probably more like seven hundred years newer."

Great. She wasn't getting it. Best to let her figure it out for herself. She wouldn't believe him if he told her, and that would be dangerous.

"Where are the nearest runes you remember seeing before?"

Wrinkling her brow at him, she raised her hand up and tipped her pointing finger over, which struck him as a quite feminine way of pointing behind him.

"Uh, I looked at some just outside the three-way fork

in the passageway when we first came in yesterday, remember? You were looking at everything with me, and then we got to the three-way fork and you asked me which way I wanted to go."

He swallowed.

"Okay, I'm going to take you out there to look at them again now, to see if you notice any changes. But Kelsey, please don't go wandering off. Promise me you'll stay with me."

She started to say something.

But he held up his hand.

Miraculously, she stopped.

"I'll explain why soon," he said. "That, I promise you. Oh, and one more thing. If we hear anyone coming, we need to run back down this hallway. We're sort of safe down here."

She smiled conspiratorially at him and narrowed her eyes.

"I knew there was something weird about this center hallway. I mean I knew it was here, but I sort of forgot about it until you took us down here just now." She looked anxiously down the hall again. "But won't they be immune to it just like you are?"

She had grown up into such a confident, competent woman. A wonderful woman. He wished he could just take her back to their time before this happened and somehow make her forget all about him so that she would be safe and happy.

But he didn't have that much control over his time traveling. He controlled when he traveled, but that was it. They controlled where he had to go in order to be able to travel—and they controlled how far back in time he traveled. Still, controlling when he traveled was a much better deal than his father had, and Tavish was grateful for that.

He sighed. He wished she weren't, but in reality Kelsey was here, and he intended to keep her as safe and happy as he could while she was here.

But they controlled what he was able to tell her.

"The 'they' I'm worried about right now are a different 'they' than the ones you heard talking a few minutes ago. But the now 'they' are mostly not immune to this hallway's influence, if that makes any sense."

She pursed her lips and nodded three times quickly, then smiled at him.

"Actually, yeah, I think I understood what you meant."

"Good. Alright, let's go."

He took her hand so that he could control how fast she walked and keep her behind him as he crept down the hallway—making as little noise as possible, especially when he got close to the opening. He was debating with himself whether he should actually take her out there where the old time people might see her.

He had barely just concluded that she really needed to understand their situation or she wouldn't stay in this safe hallway anyway, when she gasped.

"I can see the runes from here. Tavish, did somebody... Oh. Did 'they' do restoration work on the runes last night?"

He shook his head no.

"You know that's not it, Kel."

Her whole body jerked forward as if she meant to run over to the runes across the hallway and put her fingers in the grooves of them and feel how jagged the newer cuts were, compared to how smooth they'd been just yesterday.

But he held her hand tight, stopping her from going out there into danger.

She met his eyes then, and he could see the wheels turning in her mind. Her expression was only a tiny bit fearful, though. Mostly, she just looked really, really smart.

It was all he could do not to grab her in his arms and hold her close and tell her he loved her and that he would never, ever let her go, he admired her so much. And she was so much fun to be with.

"Tavish, I think I know what's going on, but humor me. I need to see some more stuff. You know, just to rule out the possibility that you're messing with me." She held up her hand to stop him from saying anything. "Normally, I would be sure you wouldn't mess with me about something this… big. But you have to admit," she gestured all around them, "that this... this is anything but normal."

"Yeah, you're right. The thing is…" He couldn't make himself say it and risk sounding stupid, so he just pointedly studied her jeans for a moment and then looked back up into her eyes.

She looked off into the corridors as if perhaps she could see a way out if she just looked hard enough.

"Well, you're in period clothing. What if you just go… find me something to wear? Heh, and that can double as showing me some more stuff. After all," she looked him in the eye again, "I know that during our time, there aren't any period women's clothes hanging around out there."

"Okay, I'll go see what I can find." He put his hand on her elbow and beseeched her with his eyes. "But Kel, you have to stay here in this hallway." Nothing else he could say would tell her any better how serious this was, so he just put all his concern for her in his eyes and prayed that she would see it.

"I will," she said, pursing her lips a little and nodding gently.

***

He had to call in a favor and tell a tall tale, but he got Kelsey some clothes that would fit and look appropriate on her during the old time. As he walked back through the underground corridors to meet up with her again, he looked around for a place for her to change.

But when he rounded the corner and entered the center pathway in the three-way fork, there was no sign of her.

Sia

After Tavish left to go find her some clothes, Kelsey leaned against the cold stone wall for a while, trying to get comfortable. But the cold got to her, so she stood back up. Casting about for a way to pass the time, she looked at the runes carved into the walls and had started tracing them with her fingers, feeling the rougher edges, when she felt a chill and then heard an unfamiliar old male voice behind her.

He was speaking a Gaelic slightly more old-fashioned than what Tavish's parents had taught her and everyone else in their faire clan—and he almost made her jump out of her skin.

"Ye are na of this time."

A jolt of adrenaline rushed through Kelsey, urging her to run. When she didn't, goosebumps rushed up her neck into her scalp and down the backs of her arms and the fronts of her legs.

She took a deep breath to calm herself and kept her back to him, tracing the runes with her fingers while she spoke to him as nonchalantly as she could in her slightly more modern Gaelic, in which she knew she could be grammatical.

"Why no, I am na. And ye are na fooled by the trick of this hallway."

He chuckled then, the way her uncle used to chuckle when she accused him of cheating at cards after his poker games, while he counted his copious winnings.

"Nay, neither of us is. Sae, can ye read then, or are ye just tracing the pretty lines?"

Loath to admit the fact that she had been just tracing the pretty lines and eager to prove that she could read them, Kelsey turned her left side toward the wall and raised her right hand to the top of the runes to point to her place as she read. This allowed her to sneak a glimpse of him.

The man's long white hair and beard cascaded down over his long white homespun linen robes. His wrinkled face was darkened by the sun, and he held in one hand a gnarled old oak walking staff. He gasped when she raised her right hand.

She looked up toward her hand to make sure there wasn't a snake up there in a crack in the wall, ready to bite her, but all she saw was her hand—oh, and her ring from Celtic University. Wow, was the shape of it something he recognized?

Just in time, her gut urged her to appear unaffected by time travel or his presence. To appear more sure of herself then she was. In short, to hide her helplessness. Still fighting the shiver she felt at the goosebumps, she went ahead and started reading the runes:

"Be happy while ye yet live, for yer time to be dead is long—"

But in a strong booming voice that caused her bones to hum, he interrupted.

"Pardon me, Priestess. I didna see yer ring afore. What hae ye come to study?"

Priestess?

But Kelsey flashed back to a line in the movie Ghostbusters—the original, not the one that came out in 2016: "If someone asks if you are a god, you always say yes." And she figured probably the same thing applies if a creepy old Druid assumes you're a Druidic priestess.

Very carefully, she didn't pause in her tracing of the runes with her fingers. Quite deliberately, she made herself not turn around and look at the man. Nonchalance was what her gut told her she needed to put on right now.

However, she was so busy putting it on that she didn't take time to consider what she would say—so she blurted out the truth.

"In my time, this place is abandonit. I've come tae see it in its former glory."

"Och, well nae, ye have come at least a thousand years ower late for that—"

Yikes, better to cut him off before he gave voice to his expectation that she just flit back in time another thousand years on her own.

"Aye. Howsoever, the castle is in use during yer time, and it should prove interesting, seeing what type o use it is being put tae, a thousand years after its prime."

"Ah. Sae that is why you hae brought Tavish, then. Tae be yer mundane guide during this time."

It now occurred to her that, as much as possible, she had better stick to the truth. It would be the easiest thing for her to remember, should she be questioned under duress. And duress seemed likely in this time. She was holding her own at the moment, just barely, but… some instinct told her to let this particular truth out.

"Forsooth, Tavish did bring me. I dinna hae the ability, myself."

The man chuckled.

"Aye, isna that a darned inconvenient limitation on us? 'Tisn't fair, that the mundanes get to do most of the time traveling."

Nonchalance. Keep up the nonchalance.

She just gave him the slightest nod in acknowledgment of what he'd said.

His footsteps went up the hallway toward the fork.

"Tavish returns, and talking tae him would be… inconvenient for me. Sae I shall leave ye tae it. Be well until we meet again, Kelsey. And when we dae, ye may call me Brian."

She felt the chill again, and then she could neither see nor hear Brian.

A few seconds later, Tavish bumped into her and dropped onto the smooth carved stone floor a lovely red wine and black tea dyed plaid overdress and a coordinating black tea linea blouse with Scottish thistles embroidered round the neckline, and a matching embroidered red wine linen snood.

"Kelsey! How did you do that?"

"Do what?"

"You know what!"

"Um, no I don't."

"You were invisible!"

"I was?"

"Come on, you know you were."

"Tavish, to me, you're the one who was invisible. I had no idea you were coming until you bumped into me just now."

They stared at each other for a few moments, apparently both waiting for the other to speak up and explain what was going on. He obviously knew something he wasn't telling her. Well, she was done telling him everything, too.

Seachd

Tavish picked up the old time clothes and rather helplessly looked around the empty corridor again, for a place for Kelsey to change. Maybe he should go out to the stables and get some hay bales to stack in the corner so she could go behind them?

But she was already taking off her leather backpack and her sweatshirt, which she stuffed inside the pack before donning the old time clothes and then putting her leather backpack on once more.

"I'll just wear it over my real clothes," she said. "That way if anybody comes, at least they won't see me naked."

"That... surprisingly practical. I have to admit, I was

seventy percent sure you would freak out when we got here to the old time."

She shrugged.

"University taught me to keep calm in strange situations. And by the way, I believe you now, about us having… gone back in time."

"Well good, because we're probably going to be here in the old time a while."

Her eyes got really big.

He rushed to explain before she panicked.

"My ring can take us back to our time, but only in this hallway. We'll arrive right back where and when we left our time. There was no one around—I'm always careful about that—but they were coming. If we go back to our time without the artifact they want, I'm afraid of what might happen to you. The artifact is probably here in this underground castle, which as you've seen is quite extensive. So we're in for a search that will certainly take a few days, if not weeks—or even months."

"What is it they want?" Her stomach growled loudly. "And I hope the people of this time have something to eat around here, because I was so excited about exploring these underground passages that I ran outside without eating breakfast first."

He looked her over to make sure her tank top and jeans weren't showing, but she'd done a good job covering them with the old time clothes. He sighed and looked up toward the fork in the corridor, then met her eyes and pointedly switched to Gaelic and went into the old time persona he put on here, while he took her by the hand and gingerly led her out.

"Well enough. There won't be anything to eat down

here. The underground castle is only used in this time to fortify the docks below, and the current laird forbids the guards to eat on duty, and as you can see there's no place to sleep either. There is an upper castle where he resides, and around it there's a substantial castle town, or castleton." He patted his sporran. "I'm employed here as a mercenary guard, so I have coinage of the time. We can buy a meal there and see about a place for you to stay. I have a bunk in the barracks."

As soon as they left the underground castle, they were inside the castleton. Kelsey turned her head every which way, and he supposed he couldn't blame her.

The buildings were close together, which meant that the streets were narrow, so all the action was close. Countless men in leather armor and carrying weapons swaggered up and down the streets along with the housewives on errands, some on their way to guard duty and others going to break for a drink at one of the many taverns. Dozens of vendors called out their wares from carts set up in the street. These were mostly edible wares, and the scent of roasting meat and baking bread and cheap wine filled the air.

Grinning a little at how preoccupied she was, Tavish bought her a 'toad in a hole' at a vendor. He didn't tell her what it was, just handed it to her.

"Here. These are good, by fegs."

His amusement grew when she took it from him and ate it without really stopping to look at it, still taking in all the sights and sounds. He let her enjoy herself, surreptitiously steering her by her elbow so that she didn't bump into anyone, and handing her his water skin when she was obviously thirsty. Watching the joy spread on her face brought him his own kind of delight.

But this wasn't a vacation.

Once she was done eating, he dug out of his sporran the drawing they had given him of the artifact they wanted and showed it to her. Couldn't hurt for her to keep an eye out. She obviously had a way of seeing things he didn't.

Her face grew concerned as she looked at the drawing.

"Forsooth Tavish, I'm in the thick o' it now, sae ye must needs tell me who 'they' are."

But he couldn't do that.

So relief coursed through him when his sparring partner in the old time—a large red-haired highlander—picked this moment to arrive and greet them, also in Gaelic. He clasped forearms with Tavish, but all the while he was smiling at Kelsey.

"Och, there ye are, Tavish. Wait, who is this?"

Tavish took advantage of the large man's distraction and grabbed the drawing from Kelsey and stuffed it back into his sporran.

"Seumas! Och, ye've found me. This is—"

"Pleased to meet ye, Seumas. I'm Kelsey." She held out her hand like the businesswoman she had become. He hoped it was obvious only to him that she meant to shake the man's hand. If anyone of the old time saw it that way, they would be scandalized.

But Seumas sparkled his green eyes and took Kelsey's proffered hand. Like one of those ridiculous portrayals of old-time men in the movies, the fool looked likely to raise it to his lips. He gave Tavish a look that dared him to stop the action, all while being apparently a complete gentleman in Kelsey's eyes, the brute.

"It is glad to know you I am, Kelsey…"

Tavish put a stop to that line of reasoning by throwing his arm around Kelsey's waist and pulling her close to him.

"Aye, Kelsey is clan, and I will thank ye to keep yer hands off her, Seumas."

He expected Kelsey to put up a fight at his protectiveness, being a modern woman and all, but she surprised him by melting into his side. Apparently she still had some sense in her.

"Tavish wis juist showing me around."

He was sure Kelsey didn't see it, but Seumas narrowed his eyes at Tavish and grinned ever so slightly before he turned to Kelsey with an open face and asked what she probably thought was an innocent question, but to him it seemed loaded.

"Do ye mean to stay here awhile, then?"

"Aye," Tavish said, "I mean to apprentice her with the weavers."

Kelsey's eyebrows wrinkled in the cutest way and her mouth hung open for a second before she recovered and got that uppity look on her face again, the look that went with her new business suits.

"The weavers?"

"Hae ye skill at the weaving?" Seumas asked her respectfully.

"I hae seen how the weaving is done," she said to Seumas while staring daggers at Tavish, "but I hae nay desire tae do it myself."

Tavish gave her a significant look.

"Och lass, did ye think Laird Malcomb would take ye on here and let ye stay for naught?"

She had to understand the old time was different, that men would be in charge of her here. He couldn't let some

77

other man grab charge of her, and she needed to realize that and help him keep her under his protection. The way she clung to him was reassuring, along these lines, but he spelled it out a bit, just to be sure she understood.

"Ye must work if ye are tae bide here at the castle while I dae ma part. Else ye must gae home to the glen with the marketing this very day."

Kelsey looked like she'd swallowed a fly.

"But couldna I do aught other than weaving? I would much rather apprentice to someone more learned."

Seumas gave Kelsey an all too charming smile and then laughed in his jolly way. Too bad there was no potbelly to go with it. The darn brute was all muscles.

"There are nae learned people here but the laird himself and his family, lass."

She pressed her lips together and then licked them, all the while wrinkling her forehead in that adorable vulnerable way that made him want to throw his arms around her and tell her everything would be fine.

"What about the laird's sons? Who teaches them?"

But Seumas beat him to it, putting his hand on her shoulder and tilting his head to the side in a way that made his long red hair tickle her cheek, so that she brushed it aside, and in so doing, touched his arm.

"Well nae, the priest does that, and ye canna mean to apprentice with him."

She went a bit limp at that, and Tavish took advantage of his arm around her waist and pulled her away from Seumas and toward the door, turning them around in the process.

"The weavers will suit ye just fine, Kel. Ye shall see."

Seumas quickly caught up and joined them, smiling at

Kelsey while he spoke to Tavish.

"And I will be seeing ye out to the sparring yard."

Now that the man was safely on the other side of him and away from Kelsey, Tavish warmly slapped his other arm around his sparring partner.

"I dinna doubt it."

But Seumas leaned forward so he could talk to Kelsey.

"So did yer husband come here to market, lass?"

Tavish tried to nip this line of enquiry in the bud. He would give her an imaginary husband, and that would keep Seumas from coming on to her. Because... Because she clearly was in over her head with an old time man. Yes, yes she was.

"Nay," said Tavish, "her husband stayed at home."

But Kelsey spoke at the same time.

"Nay, he's passed on."

Tavish couldn't help but respond with irritation to that, even though a part of him realized it would look irrational to Seumas. Why couldn't she just let him handle this? Didn't she know he was familiar with this time and knew better than her what would be acceptable now, what would be safest for her?

"And when were ye gon to tell me this?"

She put on a fake sad face for Seumas, but her finger jabbed into Tavish's rib.

"It happened but a month ago. Poor Duncan expired when a horse fell upon him."

Tavish crossed himself, as did Seumas, and Kelsey had the sense to imitate them as she prattled on about her imaginary husband's death for five minutes. Finally, she got to why she was here.

"I was after a bit o' distraction when they did say

would I come along to market—"

Here, she put her hand on Tavish's face in that way she had that always melted his heart.

"—and perhaps to visit with any clan at the castle."

Hold on, he could make her crazy story serve his purpose. His eyes held Seumas's while he spoke to Kelsey.

"It's as well. Only *clan* ought to console you during this time."

This brought them to the weaver's shop up top in the castle town, which was bustling with people who had come from far and wide—mostly by boat at nearby Port Patrick—to buy and sell goods before winter set in.

Tavish rapped on the door.

"Hey ho, the weaver shop."

The door banged open and four well-dressed blond children greeted them with laughter while they chided and tickled and poked each other, all the while running about in circles and finally down the lane.

Tavish, Seumas, and Kelsey went inside the shop, where they saw a grey haired woman weaver at her loom, a blonde woman about their age working wet strands of the flax plant into threads, and two men who were probably the women's husbands, one gray-haired and one blond, pounding on soaking flax plants to separate them into strands. They were all weavers, so of course all their clothes were finely made and new. Verra respectable, Tavish noted with satisfaction.

The blond woman working the wet strands set them down and came to the door with a question in her brown eyes.

"What can I dae to help ye?"

"It is we who will be helping ye. Kelsey has come to

apprentice."

The woman looked Kelsey up and down.

"A bit old for an apprentice, be ye not?"

Tavish gave Kelsey a grudging nod, because her story made more sense now. To support it, he put his arm around her in comfort.

"My clanswoman has lost her husband and seeks some distraction these weeks while she is here tae visit me."

The woman gave Kelsey a comforting smile and reached for her hand, which Kelsey slowly gave her while looking back at Tavish with near panic in her eyes. The woman led Kelsey over to her work.

"We could use the help. I'll show ye how tae separate the strands."

"See ye at supper, Kel."

And with that, Tavish quickly walked off, before Kelsey could introduce anymore awkward conversation.

Seumas was still there, though.

"Your clanswoman is a pretty one."

"Aye."

"Mind if I—"

Tavish turned toward his sparring partner.

"Ye had better not."

The kilted warrior grinned at him.

"If yer wanting tae mak some time with her, then whyever did ye put her in with the weavers?"

"I am na wanting tae mak time with her."

The huge red-haired highlander laughed and clapped him on the back, hard.

"Ye can fool yerself, MacGregor, but ye will na fool me."

"I am na fooling myself. I did na want her tae come

here, but now that she's here, 'tis my duty to protect her. She'll be safe with the weavers. And they'll keep her busit."

But Seumas kept laughing and patting Tavish's back.

"Ye mark my words, MacGregor. Ye will be sorry they keep her sae busit."

Ochd

"Glad tae know ye, Kelsey. I'm Eileen."

Kelsey tried not to have a sour face. It wasn't Eileen's fault Tavish had dumped her in this thirteenth century sweatshop. Maybe if she just left this room, she could catch up with him, and… No, the stubborn arse would just bring her back here.

"Hello," she said to Eileen as brightly as she could. "It looks like ye need a lot of help."

The blonde woman's brown eyes lit up with a smile, and she bent over a bit in laughter.

"Aye, and this weaving is na the half of it. Ye saw my wild ones just now, running oot."

Eileen had a warm manner, and soon Kelsey was doing her best to help the woman.

The work didn't demand very much mental activity at

all though, so while she worked, Kelsey considered her options. Chasing after Tavish was out, but just leaving and going back into the underground castle? No, if Seumas was down there, then other people might be down there, and while they might know Tavish, she was a stranger. Who knew what they might do to her.

But Eileen was understandably curious and asked questions as the two of them combed flax into thread.

"I'm sorry about yer husband. Were ye married long, and hae ye wee ones?"

Kelsey pretended it was Tavish she was being asked about, and answered with details of their prior relationship. She'd had other boyfriends, but if she was honest with herself, he was the only one who… She didn't let herself think about that.

"We were together four verra good years filled with love and laughter, and nay, no children."

"Aw, sad I am for ye on both counts, from the loss of yer husband to the lack of children."

Lack of children was the least of it. Now that she knew why Tavish had disappeared, her feelings were even more hurt than they had been freshman year at college.

A lump formed in Kelsey's throat as she looked around at the intact stone walls of their castleyard stall, the chinks freshly reinforced against the wind with wet straw, the amazing loom busy weaving a plaid.

If she had been the one to time travel instead of Tavish, she would have shared this with him. He'd known how fascinated she was with the past and how much she would've loved to be involved with this sooner. Obviously he didn't… no, obviously he hadn't felt the same way about her.

But she gave Eileen her bravest face.

"Dinna fash for me."

Eileen gave her a kind smile, and then her eyes grew full of mischief.

"I see that yer clan man is fond of ye."

Huh? Kelsey searched Eileen's eyes for sties, or glaucoma, or cataracts. Hm. They seemed to be clear and unimpeded.

"Ye think Tavish is interestit in me? It does na seem sae tae me. After all, he dumpit me here and ran off tae hae fun with his friend."

Eileen laughed hard at that.

"He did na run off tae hae fun."

"Aye, he did. He and Seumas were talking aboot sparring with their swords."

"Ye haven't spent any time at a castle, have ye?"

"Nay, does it show, then?"

The weaver bit her knuckle, apparently to keep from laughing anymore at Kelsey's expense.

"Aye, it does, for this whole place is naught but a fancy barracks for soldiers, ye ken. They spar most of ivery day sae that they can fight when they're needed, or else the laird does na feed them."

"I thank ye for the explanation. I sort of wonderit about all the shapely men wandering aboot with swords."

Eileen must have been disposed toward laughing, for she did it some more, and it didn't seem to take much effort. Kelsey also noticed that one of the male weavers kept eyeing Eileen and talking about her to the other.

But Eileen's brown eyes were still full of mischief.

"Nay, I dae think Tavish is sweet on ye. Protective. I did see the way he lookit aboot the shop in an attempt tae suss oot any trouble that might be lingering, before he left ye here. He is na a relative, is he."

It wasn't a question, but Kelsey answered it anyway. Semi honestly.

"Nah, he is na, and we playit kissing games when we were children. But even if he's not off having fun, he's off me, and has been for years." She'd had enough of this line of questioning, and she remembered something about how the best defense is a strong offense, so Kelsey lowered her voice and leaned in toward Eileen, squinting her eyes conspiratorially. "So I guess that's yer husband ower thare?"

Eileen leaned in too, but her jaw dropped, and she quickly dipped her chin so that she was looking at Kelsey almost through her own forehead.

"Fergus? Nay, my own husband did pass six months ago."

"Oh. I'm sorry for yer loss an all. I just thought from the way he was looking at ye that the twa o ye were marriit. I'd say he thinks ye are headit that way."

Good, Eileen blushed. Now to keep her on the defense so she would quit making Kelsey think of things that she could only regret thinking about. Expensive notions, when it came to getting her feelings hurt. Again.

Kelsey gave the weaver woman an appraising look. Eileen's clothes were modest, of course. Everyone knew that was just the way things were back in this time. Women couldn't seem too forward or they would be mistaken for whores, much more so than in modern times. But Eileen was attractive, an eight without trying, who could be a nine if she put in some effort.

"Yer een are still free o wrinkles, Eileen. Ye can dae

better than Fergus. Don't ye think ye should try?"

Eileen's attractive face scrunched up. Yeah, Eileen was way better looking than Kelsey herself. If she scrunched her face up like that, she would just look ugly. On Eileen it was cute and made Kelsey want to help her. The woman didn't appreciate her own beauty.

"Better?" said the weaver, "How dae ye mean?"

"I mean, you're a craftswoman, and there's no shame in that, but isn't there a single man who has more status than a weaver does, and who you have a chance with?"

Eileen discreetly looked over at Fergus and then back at Kelsey. She still kept her voice low.

"Aye, there is."

"A man who ye like and who might like ye?"

Eileen not only stopped working, but also took a strand of her blonde hair and started twirling it around her finger.

"Hmmmmm."

The way the woman hummed made Kelsey's cheeks ache with a smile. She made a conscious effort not to laugh and attract the attention of the men.

"I thought sae. Now when's the neist time ye are gaun'ae see him?"

"This evening at supper, I suppose."

"How aboot if ye pinch yer cheeks an crush some berries tae put on yer lips, put on yer finest clothes, an make some conversation with him?"

Eileen quit twirling her hair and got back to combing the flax into thread.

"I don't really have anything in common with him, Kelsey."

"Of course ye dae."

Eileen stopped working again and put her hands on her

hips.

"Verra well, if ye know sae much, what could we possibly hae in common?"

Kelsey met Eileen's eyes and very pointedly looked at Fergus and then at their flax work and started working again, waiting for Eileen to start again too. And giving her time to think of an answer.

The weaver paused only a few moments before she nodded and started work again, but it was enough. Inspiration struck Kelsey.

"Ye both live here in this marvelous castle town, do ye not?"

Eileen nodded at her, putting more effort into the work as she spoke.

"Aye, we do, but everyone here does, sae that doesn't give us any special connection."

Kelsey met Eileen's eyes and tsked.

"But it does give ye things tae talk aboot: the weather, if naught else, but ye also know all the same people and see all the same merchants and ships, eat the same foods, have heard the same stories growing up, and the same rumors. Ye have all things in common, really. I envy you. My parents and I movit tae a new town when I was fourteen, and I had tae start all ower again with people who did na hae a thing in common with me at all, not even the weather. If it had na been for Tavish…" Ugh. She had done it to herself this time. She needed to get off that topic posthaste. "Sae aye, ye can speak with this more successful man." There. She'd made a good case for Eileen to step out and make something of herself.

But the weaver seemed to know a bit herself, about a good offense.

"Ye movit tae a new place ootside o a castle with juist yer parents and no yer whole clan? Thare has tae be a tale in that."

Now Kelsey had done it. Put her foot squarely in her mouth. For a moment, she considered toppling something so the men would come over. But it was going to be a long day, and there was no way Eileen would let this go.

"It is na much of a tale, for sooth. Da took work with a... merchant. He's good at... selling things. Soon, everyone in our clan's area had the merchant's goods, but Da enjoyit the money he made doing this work. When the merchant offerit him the same work in another place—and also offerit tae pay sae Da and his family could move there—Da acceptit."

Eileen smiled at her sympathetically.

"So ye left all that ye knew. And ye were fourteen? And then ye met Tavish?"

Kelsey gave her new friend an exasperated smile.

"Aye, now can we stop making all things be aboot Tavish?"

Eileen's smile turned mischievous again.

"I daresay that for ye, all things already are aboot him."

And round and round they went, but it passed the time. Meanwhile, for the first half of her workday, Kelsey meant to kill Tavish when he came to see her for supper. He had dragged her out of an underground castle—incredible, marvelous, and secret—in order to dump her in the weaver shop and make her work all day? And it was hard, boring work. She'd had no idea linen was so difficult to make in pre-industrial times.

But after a late morning break for bangers and mash, the scholar in Kelsey started to appreciate what an opportunity this was.

By the decorative patterns Eileen's coworker was weaving into the linen, Kelsey knew this was the 13th century. Her eyes began to drink in all the details of the weaver shop, from the construction of the loom to the way the people dressed and even the game the children played in the corner during their short breaks from helping with the work—one sort of like jacks but with little stones.

Kelsey asked and was told where to go relieve herself, and once she had privacy, she put her phone in the hanging cradle of one of her huge linen sleeves and cut a hole in the linen next to it, just big enough for the camera lens. By crossing her arms just so, she could look natural while using it.

She carefully snapped about a hundred photos on her short walk from the privy back to the weaver's shop— mostly of the intact castle and its courtyard, but also of the way people were dressed and their various weapons. She could blow the pictures up on her computer once she got home, and hopefully see all the fine details of craftsmanship.

When she got back inside the shop, she snapped one of the loom and the way the woman who worked it was sitting at it. And then she turned her phone off to save the battery and got back to her hard, boring work.

After an early afternoon break—for more bangers and mash—she started to worry. What if something happened to Tavish? Would she be stuck here for the rest of her life?

Her mind went back to Brian. Could he help her? He'd implied that he wasn't able to time travel himself, but that he knew others who could...

But Brian was an unknown. She didn't know if she

could trust him. Tavish was a safer bet, and it sounded like his time traveling ability was dependent on whoever 'they' were. And 'they' wanted that artifact. So shouldn't she be looking for it, not wasting time here in this shop?

~*~

It was getting dark when Tavish finally came in the door to get her for supper. Anxious to have a word with him, she dropped her work, jumped up, and rushed to meet him at the door. But she was puzzled when he wouldn't lock arms with her when she offered. He just scooped up her leather backpack and headed out the door.

She rushed to keep up with him.

"So do we eat dinner in the castle? Where am I going to sleep? Will I get my own room, or do I have to bunk with others?"

He kept quiet until he had walked them the long way out of the castle wall and up a barren hill, where no one was around. When he stopped and turned to look at her, there was fear in his eyes.

"What do you mean to do with all the pictures you took today?"

She couldn't ever remember seeing him afraid before.

"No one noticed I was taking them, Tavish. I mean, I guess you saw me, but no one else knows what a phone is, so they don't know I did it."

He grimaced and looked away for a moment. When he turned back to her, the fear was gone, replaced by... determination. He spoke softly, so that she had to strain to hear.

"Let's assume for right now that they didn't notice."

"They didn't."

He put his hand out in front of him palm down and

lowered it toward the ground.

"Fine. Given the best scenario where no one here knows anything is amiss, you do understand that once we get home, you can't post those photos online for your university colleagues to see, don't you?"

Really? Here they were back in the thirteenth century, and he was worried about her posting photos online when they got back home?

"Come on, Tavish. I know that."

He looked her in the eye then, beseeching her with his deep brown eyes.

"Are you sure?"

She let herself get lost in his eyes for so long, he finally raised an eyebrow in inquiry. Oh yeah, their conversation.

"Of course I'm sure. Come on, why do you think I'm so stupid?"

He pursed his perfectly shaped, manly lips.

"Because you were awfully insistent about posting the photos you took of the client's property back in our time, and I doubt very much he wants that."

She nodded to the side and threw her hand up a little bit.

"Okay. You have a point."

He grabbed both of her upper arms and drew her toward him, causing a different kind of goosebumps to run all the way down to her toes.

"This isn't the debate team, Kelsey. This could be the death of us. Do you see that now?"

"Tavish, yes, I do, okay?"

"So what are you going to do with these pictures?"

"I just want to have them for my own knowledge."

"Do you promise?"

"Yes, I promise."

"And isn't your phone one of those android phones that automatically upload to Google Pictures?"

"Yeah, but no one can see my Google Pictures unless I share them."

"Are you sure about that?"

"Pretty sure."

"Kel, make darn sure, okay?"

"Right now?"

He looked around.

"No, not here out in the open. Let's go sit on the grass between those rocks."

Once they were seated side by side, he took out another drawing he had in his sporran and held it in his lap where they could both look at it. She used their tableaux as lookers at a drawing as a cover for playing with her phone.

"Okay. Now I'm 100% sure that my camera won't upload these to Google Pictures."

"Good. Now let's just pray that no one did notice you taking them."

No one here could possibly understand what it would mean for her to be aiming her elbow subtly and casually at things and pausing for a second, right? But Tavish acted so worried about it that his paranoia was rubbing off on her. Add to that her keen awareness that she was dependent on him to get home, and now her body was once again urging her to run somewhere, blood pumping and heart racing.

"Let's go to dinner," he said, getting up and giving her a hand to help her up.

"All right," she agreed, taking his hand.

But when she got up, she was trembling, and she clung to his hand in real need of support for a few seconds longer.

His support was unhesitating, firm, and sure. He patiently stood there waiting for her to steady herself.

Before she realized it, she was looking up into his eyes, searching for reassurance.

And it was there, right there on his face: loyalty, devotion even—the promise that he would never leave her behind—

"Och, there ye are, Tavish. Laird Malcomb sent me oot after ye, says ye best come quick if ye want tae gae tae Bangor with us on the morrow."

Seumas bent over a bit and put his hands on his knees, gulping air.

"Aye?" said Tavish. "Well then, see gin ye can keep up wi us."

He kept hold of her hand and started running in the direction where Seumas had come from, laughing the whole way. She knew he wasn't running his fastest, because she kept up with him easily. At first.

But when Seumas passed him, Tavish dropped her hand and tossed her leather backpack to her, then went running to try and catch up to Seumas, but he didn't. Panting a bit, the two men stopped at the castle town gate and turned to look at her.

"I'm coming, I'm coming," she assured them as she walked more sedately, with the pack on her back, because she was approaching the castle and didn't want to trip over her long skirts where anyone could see. Her slow approach allowed her to appreciate the beauty of the sunset behind them, off the cliff and over the sparkling sea next to Ireland.

They both offered their arms to her, and she took both,

so that the three of them were walking through the town in a linked chain with her in the middle.

"Another merchant ship wanting a guard tae Bangor?" said Tavish.

"Aye, and no juist any merchant ship, but Donnell's again."

Kelsey pulled on both of their arms in order to get them to quit talking over her head. "Sae ye hae guarded merchant ships?"

"Sure, thon is most of the work we dae here," Tavish told her.

"Well, whit dae ye guard from, pirates?"

She'd been grinning a silly grin because she'd said that in fun, but Tavish and Seumas turned serious faces to her. This time it was Seumas who spoke.

"Aye, there are pirates aboot betimes. 'Tis no a laughing matter, lass."

She smirked at him.

"Nay, that canna be true."

"Aye, lass, it is."

Kelsey looked to Tavish for an admission that they were having fun with her, pulling her leg. What she saw in his eyes surprised her. He was serious. But more than that, he looked worried again. And determined.

"They've never yet gotten the best of us, mostly because we know what we're doing. Donnell runs a tight ship, aye Seumas?"

The red haired giant pursed his lips and nodded yes to Kelsey.

"Aye, that he does, indeed. We hae only been boarded twice, and both times we killed every one of those sorry MacDonalds. The world would be a far better place if they would all die out, ye ken. Why, we ought tae…"

What? Kelsey put a hand up in front of Seumas's face and waved it to get his attention.

"Wait a minute. Ye mean tae tell me the pirates are other Scots?"

Seumas and Tavish exchanged a look over her head.

For a moment, it was all she could do not to stomp on their feet, but she forced herself to be polite. Only because she was walking through a medieval town—in a backward time when women had to be even more careful than in the twenty first century.

This brought them to the oak plank door of the aboveground castle that in her time had been long destroyed, only lines of different colored stone in the ground, not even sticking up an inch above the wild grass. The castle was huge.

Seumas dropped her arm to hold the door, and Tavish put his hand on her lower back and escorted her inside.

The three of them entered directly into a huge dining hall with vaulted ceilings complete with iron candelabras hanging from the eaves. A hundred planked wooden tables stood in three large concentric squares, and the head table where Laird Malcomb sat with his lady and his sons was on the far side of the room.

Laird Malcomb saw them.

"Ah, there ye are, Tavish. Dae come sup at my table, and bring yer lovely clanswoman."

Tavish raised his other arm in greeting and then left his hand on her lower back the whole way across the great hall. His casual touch was reassuring. There were many single men in the room, judging by the lack of women by their sides, and she could imagine them all leering at her.

Instead, they were measuring up Tavish.

Oh, there was Eileen across the room, sitting with a very handsome blond man who wasn't Fergus. Kelsey waited until she looked up, and then waved a little. When Eileen smiled at her, she gave the weaver a thumbs up. At the last second, she worried a bit. Would a thumbs up send the same message now as it did in her time?

But yeah. Whew, Eileen smiled back and raised her eyebrows a little before turning back to her handsome dinner partner.

Seumas must've seen Kelsey wave, because he spoke to her then while he gave the couple his own wave, which was much more enthusiastic than hers.

"Aha. The bonnie weaver ye are apprenticed tae is eating with my brother Alfred."

Alfred raised his cup in a toast to Seumas then, with a smile and a wink that Kelsey figured must be about some in-joke between them.

Tavish took her on across the dining hall, and when they drew near the head table, Laird Malcomb gestured at three seats down the head table from him. Some servants pulled out velvet upholstered chairs for them as he talked.

Tavish steered Kelsey into the chair closest to Lord Malcomb and sat down between her and Seumas. He rested his arm on the top of her chair, and she was acutely aware of how near he was, without quite touching her.

A woman sat at Kelsey's other hand, clearly the wife or relative of the man next to her, because their plaids matched.

But Laird Malcomb was addressing her.

"It is well thon we hae all met ye, Kelsey MacGregor."

She nodded her head at him.

"I thank ye, Laird Malcomb."

The laird turned his eyes.

"Tavish."

"Aye, Laird?"

"On the morn, ye are tae join Seumas's crew agin aboard Donnell's ship doon in Port Patrick, for tae sail ower Bangor way."

Tavish bowed his head the slightest.

"Aye, Laird. I wish tae bring Kelsey along, Laird."

At the mention of her going along with Tavish and Seumas to Ireland and not being left behind here, Kelsey relaxed from a stiffness she hadn't realized was in her body. Her head nudged Tavish's arm, and it dropped down and wrapped around her shoulders, making her whole body hum with the thrill of his touch.

Laird Malcomb fixed his stern eyes on her.

"Is there some aught your clanswoman can add tae the trip, Tavish?"

"Aye, Laird, there is. Kelsey can dae sums."

There was a general tittering. The woman next to Kelsey looked at her with interest.

Laird Malcomb raised an eyebrow, clearly enjoying the theatrical aspect of this announcement.

"Can she, now?"

Kelsey stood up, feeling Tavish's arm ever so slowly release her, then linger on her hand and give a reassuring squeeze.

"Aye, Laird Malcomb. If I can hae some aught to write on, I'll then show ye."

Laird Malcomb turned to some servants.

"There, lad, bring us the writing desk from my study."

A boy of about ten rushed off out the door.

Kelsey squeezed Tavish's hand back, then let go and made her way up to the head of the table and stood behind Laird Malcomb, waiting.

The laird continued speaking, loudly enough so that everyone at their table could hear, and he continued to speak to Tavish about Kelsey, even though she was standing right next to him.

"How can the MacGregors afford tae teach a woman her sums, then?"

Tavish laughed.

"She's very clever, Laird Malcomb. She taught herself by watching. None of us fashit. Quite handy it is, having another soul aboot who can run the numbers."

Tavish winked at her.

She just shrugged with an odd little grin on her face, unsure if it was nerves or smugness, and trying not to gush in front of all these people at how proud he looked of her. She happened to glance over at Eileen right then, and the weaver shook her head with a big smile on her face before turning back to converse with Alfred. Okay, smugness it was. May as well have fun with this. It would be much easier than the demonstrations her professors had assigned. Piece of cake.

Meanwhile, the boy ran in with the writing desk, looking all around for someplace to set it down.

Laird Malcomb got up and walked over to a side table. "Set it up here, lad."

He stood aside and watched the boy set down and open a large worn wooden box on top of the table so that it resembled one of those old-fashioned desks with the shelves in front. It was obviously old, but it was also lovingly used—well oiled, without any signs of splintering, drying out, or rot. Inside were folded pieces of what must've been vellum, as well as several quills and an inkwell.

But what caught Kelsey's eye were the decorations on the outside of the writing desk. The Celtic runes were lovely of course, but even more alarmingly, they declared it the property of the king of Alba. There was more, but she could no longer see it now that the writing desk was open. The inside was just as well cared for, but sadly free of runes.

"There we are, my dear. Now dae come sit doon and shew us."

Kelsey tore her eyes away from the desk just in time to see the laird gesture at the chair someone had kindly pulled over, and all she could do was hope she hadn't missed a beat as she sat down, opened the inkwell, and dipped one of the quills in it.

Laird Malcomb's hand hovered near hers the whole time she handled the quill.

But these quills were simple, compared with the fancy art ones she had used in her studies. She looked up at him expectantly.

The laird cleared his throat.

"Verra well. Let us try this sum."

Kelsey pulled out one of the sheets of vellum. It was a rougher piece of deer hide than those she'd used at university, but just as fine and pliable, while at the same time sturdy. She poised the quill over the top of the vellum and turned to look at the laird.

He posed dramatically for a moment as The Thinker, with his fist to his forehead, and everyone in the hall laughed. He smiled—probably at the pleasure of all their attention—and then boomed out in a voice big enough to reach the farthest corner, pacing with a sway of his great kilt as he spoke, quite the orator.

"A laird went tae battle with a hundrit men. Half o them were marrit, and their wives did come along, tae cook for the men, an tae stitch up their wounds. Along the way, first five men joinit them, and then six more, and then seven more beside, half o all these with their wives. Well enough, how many mouths did the laird have tae feed?"

Kelsey felt the laird bending over her shoulder as she did the math. She glanced over at the laird's wife and wrinkled her brow in apology, and then went back to work.

"He had one hundred and seventy seven mouths tae feed, Laird Malcomb."

He bent down to check her math, and she scooted her chair back, again looking over at his lady. This time she ventured a smile at the woman.

The woman nodded, and Kelsey breathed easier.

"Verra good," said Laird Malcomb, "I am impressit."

Kelsey started to get up. Everyone else was eating and drinking, and she saw that there was food on her plate. Roasted duck, if her nose was right.

"But stay a while. This is the only show we hae this evening, sae let us see if yer ability with numbers goes beyond sums, an if sae, how far."

Kelsey only dared look at her plate a moment more, where Tavish gave her a soft look of encouragement, and then she scooted back up to the desk, inked the quill once more, and poised it over the vellum.

Laird Malcomb paced while he spoke.

"Two thirds o the laird's men were woundit in battle. O the wounded, ivery tenth died. In addition, a fever overtook the camp at night on the way back tae their castle an took ivery fifth person remaining. How many returnit tae the castle?"

Kelsey paused with her quill over the vellum.

"That depends, Laird Malcomb."

"Aye?"

"Aye, Laird Malcomb."

"Upon what, my dear?"

"The eighteen men and nine wives who joinit the laird along the way, did they who survivit among them gae back tae their homes, or did they gae tae the castle? I'm thinking they went back tae their homes, because they really wouldn't be returning tae the castle, now would they?"

Laird Malcomb threw his head back and laughed.

"Tavish, ye hae the right of it. Your clan's Kelsey is far too clever."

"Begging yer pardon, Laird Malcomb," said Seumas, standing behind his empty plate at the table and wiping his mouth with a large linen napkin, "but should na we give her some merchant items tae sum? After all, while these battle sums are entertaining, it is hoped that she will only need tae dae merchant sums in Bangor on the morrow."

Still chuckling, Laird Malcomb held his palm out toward Seumas.

"Nay, my guid man. Sums are the least o what she just did. She has the gift o knowing when someone is leading another astray, as I tryit tae dae with the men who joinit the laird along the way tae battle." He looked over at a man at the table. "She has a good head for business, Donnell. She will be a good asset for ye in Ireland upon the morrow." And then to Kelsey, he said, "Gae on and eat yer food now, lass. Ye've earned it."

"I thank ye, Laird."

Kelsey hurried over to her seat to do as she'd been told.

Tavish and Seumas both stood when she got there, but a servant pulled out her chair and seated her.

Still standing, Tavish patted her on the shoulder.

"Please stay here. I'll be back straight away."

"All right."

The spot where he had tapped her shoulder still glowed with his warmth all the while Seumas made small talk in Tavish's absence. She did her best to keep up with it and be polite while she ate.

"I truly admire yer cleverness, Kelsey. I couldna hae done those sums better myself. But ye are not only clever. Ye make a fine figure of a woman as well."

"Why thank ye, Seumas. I admired the way ye gave Tavish a run for his money earlier."

"It was a good race, was na it?"

"Aye, verra close, but you did come oot the victor."

The big red-haired man was quiet for a moment, and Kelsey thought the conversation was over, but then he continued it, and she kept being polite.

"I have na seen the MacGregor holdings, but dare I say ye could hae as good a life here, in Laird Malcomb's Castle."

She appreciatively took in the grand hall in its present well-maintained state, all the wood polished, all the stonework scrubbed, and fresh candles everywhere, their smoke escaping through artfully placed holes in the roof while fires roared in two huge fireplaces.

"'Tis verra safe here, lass. With all of us aboot, no one is going to set upon ye. And even when we are oot to battle, these walls will protect ye, the walls and yer women's arrows."

She lifted her pewter goblet and sipped her wine, using the gesture to look discreetly and see if Tavish was on his way back to her.

"I can see that is true."

Seumas sipped his wine as well and started to relax into his seat, but when she set her goblet down, he set his down and looked at her earnestly.

"Laird Malcomb does give us some aught each evening—be times someone of talent such as yerself, but more often than not we get music, and dancing."

His earnestness made her giggle a little.

"Och, it could be fun to live here, that is sure."

Kelsey shared a little smile with Seumas.

General conversation had picked up in the hall, so she was no longer the center of attention. Tavish had made sure she was going along to Bangor tomorrow, and her food wasn't too cold.

Things were looking up.

Naoi

Things were looking down.

The longer Kelsey was here in the old time, the higher the chance of her modern sensibilities coming out. She was doing a great job so far, but it was only a matter of time before some man said something—or did something—and she went off on him. And then all hell would break loose.

He had to prevent that, and the only way was to keep her close to him. And she needed to be with him during waking hours anyway so that he could take her with him if some Druid ran into him and sent him to some other time.

Or place. He couldn't imagine them patiently waiting for him to get her.

He had to find the artifact they wanted as soon as possible so that he could get her back home where she'd be safe. And now there would be a trip to Bangor tomorrow. The whole day would be wasted.

Good, the weaver lady was still at supper.

"Pray pardon an interruption?" said Tavish to the table at large.

The big kilted warrior she was sitting with looked up first and then smiled and stood.

"Not at all. Ye are sitting at the laird's table with my brother Seumas, so ye must be important." He reached out with his sword arm, and Tavish clasped forearms with him. "I'm Alfred. Tae what dae we owe the honor?"

Tavish smiled at the weaver woman when she caught his eye, but she was obviously under Alfred's protection, so he addressed his comments to the warrior.

"My clanswoman apprenticed with yer lovely supper partner today, and I've come tae see if she can share her accommodation with her, or find her an appropriate place to sleep."

Alfred deferred to the weaver, who smiled at Tavish again.

"I dae thank ye for bringing Kelsey tae us. She is a lot of help. My children and I still hae my husband's house in Castleton, and I would be happy tae make a home for her while she's here visiting ye, Tavish MacGregor. And please, dae call me Eileen."

"Och. I thank ye sae much," he said to Eileen, and then he spoke mostly to Alfred. "Once ye hae finished eating, will ye please come and get us? O course I will see Kelsey tae Eileen's house safely, and I will pick her up at dawn for our trip to Bangor."

"Aye," said Alfred, "'twill be my pleasure."

"Eileen," said Tavish, "I am sorry for the loss of Kelsey's help on the morrow. If there ever be aught I can dae for ye, I would be pleased if ye made it known to me."

Eileen was looking across the room when she answered him.

"Sure and I will."

Tavish locked forearms again with Alfred.

"We will be at our table."

"We will see ye soon."

Tavish was almost back to the head table when he saw Kelsey and Seumas talking with their heads close together, smiling and laughing over his empty chair. The couple on the other side of Kelsey had left, so Tavish pulled out the woman's chair by Kelsey's side.

At the movement, she turned her head, and when she saw it was him, she turned her whole body.

"I was starting to think ye fell— I mean, that something was amiss."

He laughed.

"Nothing so dramatic, just arranging yer sleeping quarters with Eileen. It appears I've missed a bunch o fun here, though."

She smiled and glanced at Seumas.

"Yer sparring partner was just filling me in aboot the standard of entertainment in this hall. He says there is something tae see or hear or dae ivery night. Right, Seumas?"

Seumas nodded to her and then met Tavish's eyes over her head, looking more like a doctor or a preacher than a warrior, his eyes had such softness in them.

"Aye, I did tell the lass what a fine life she might hae here, did she wish tae stay."

Uh oh. Here it came. Tavish searched Kelsey's face for any sign of fear at the idea of remaining here—or anger at the idea of a stranger suggesting it, but he didn't see any. She seemed content, relaxed, and enjoying herself. How weird. He opened his mouth to ask her about that, discreetly, but she spoke first.

"Sae what sort o sums will I need tae dae for Donnell tomorrow?"

"Och," said Tavish, "Donnell is Laird Malcomb's steward of ships. We will take a boatload o cow leather and vellum ower, and then we will bring all manner o goods back here from the huge port in Bangor, Ireland."

She winked at him, and smiled in amusement.

"All manner o goods, eh?"

He raised his eyebrows at her. For someone with a degree in Celtic artwork, she didn't know much about the Celts and the extent of their trading.

"Aye, spices from India, tea from China, rugs from Persia, cedar chests from Lebanon, ye name it, he imports it. Yer task will be tae make sure everything is present after the loaders get finished."

She wrinkled her brow and lowered her chin and dropped her mouth open in the cutest gesture he'd ever seen. She put her hand on his knee and pushed. Hard.

"Tavish. That's a huge task ye hae signed me up for. How am I going tae get all that done?"

He tried to stop himself, but he chuckled a little at her expression. But at the touch of her hand on his knee through his kilt, he took a napkin off the table and put it in his lap, gesturing for Seumas to give him his wine.

"Thank ye, Seumas." He drank it all down, grateful for its instant calming effect. "Kelsey, ye won't hae tae dae it all yerself. We'll help ye. But ye see it was a long stretch, getting Laird Malcomb tae let ye come along." And then he stared into her eyes, willing her to understand what he meant, despite what he had to say in front of others. "And I know how ye hae always wanted tae see Ireland, aye?"

She sighed, but she popped her eyes wide open for a moment, just for Tavish to see, then slumped in her chair.

"Aye."

Seumas spoke to her, but he met Tavish's eyes over her head again.

"There, there, lass. Ye don't hae tae dae it. We men can manage on our own. There will be other trips to Ireland, many of them, if ye dae stay here. Ye can go another time, when ye are more accustomed tae this place, and tae our ways."

Tavish locked eyes with Seumas to show he meant business.

"Nay, she's going."

Seumas raised his eyebrows at Tavish.

"Aye? Is that the way of it, then?"

Kelsey scooted her chair back, and the wooden legs made a loud scraping noise on the stone floor. When the two of them turned to look at her, she had a twinkle in her eye and she was smiling.

"It's all right Seumas. I dae want tae go. I'm looking forward tae it."

Seumas kept looking at Tavish.

"Well then, things are set. For the morrow."

Tavish nodded at Seumas, then turned to smile at

Kelsey.

She gave him a hopeful smile, then followed his gaze over toward Alfred and Eileen's table.

He was relieved to see them walking toward him.

Deich

Kelsey went to meet Eileen when she saw her coming, and she threw her arms around the woman and gave her a big hug.

"Thank ye, thank ye, thank ye!"

Eileen laughed, but she hugged Kelsey back while Alfred went over to speak with his brother and Tavish.

"Och, wait till ye see the place before ye thank me sae much. Thare are four children livin thare, ye know."

Kelsey broke out of the hug and made a dismissive gesture with her hand, looking over to make sure the men were out of earshot and lowering her voice against those still seated nearby overhearing.

"Ay, thank ye for the place tae stay an aw, but I meant thank ye for comin along juist now."

Eileen cast a worried glance over at the men.

"Och? What's the matter?"

Kelsey smirked to let Eileen know it wasn't danger she had fled, but annoyance.

"As if it wasn't enough that Tavish was always butting intae my business, now Seumas is finding the need tae dae sae as well."

But instead of commiserating with her, Eileen got a big grin on her face. What was up with that? Kelsey looked over at the men again.

"Canna ye dae better than Seumas's brother? I mean, he's handsome, but gin he's anythin like Seumas, that's a bit owerbearing, ye ken?"

Eileen bit her knuckle again, and only spoke once she'd contained her laughter.

"Kelsey, Alfred and Seumas are Laird Malcomb's nephews, and the laird's sons are marriit now. Sae thare really is na much better we could dae."

"We?"

Kelsey looked over at the men yet again. Now that Eileen mentioned it, the brothers' linen shirts were a little finer than those of the other warriors in the hall. Their kilted plaids were similar to the laird's. They wore fine brooches that might even be signets of some kind. When she turned back, Eileen was smirking.

"Well, ye are in need of a husband."

"I did na say I needed one, just that I did lose one."

"'Tis the same difference."

Kelsey crossed her arms to show that she wouldn't be persuaded.

"Perchance around here it is, but not where I hail from."

Eileen was giving her a puzzled look, but Kelsey nodded sideways, where the men were coming over.

Alfred found his way to Eileen's side instantly and offered his arm.

"Let us gae an get yer children, and then ma brother and I and Tavish will see ye home."

She smiled up at him and took his arm.

Tavish and Seumas were both looking at Kelsey intently and moving forward as if they meant to come over and take charge and tell her what to do once more.

She headed them off at the pass, stepping between them and grabbing both of their arms again, just like when they came in. Acting like the three of them had been playmates since they were little, she kept her voice cheerful and light, like this was all in fun.

"Come on. I'm dyin tae see where Alfred put Eileen's children."

In front of them, Alfred laughed.

"Na place thon interesting, juist in the nursery with Maw. Howsoever, now I wish I had stuffit them intae one o the old castle's dungeons."

Everyone laughed, including some of the diners at nearby tables.

Kelsey looked into Tavish's deep brown eyes, and they were aglow with at least as much excitement as she felt. He dropped her arm, raised his eyebrows at her, and gave her a 'Go on' nod toward Alfred with his chin.

Kelsey dropped Seumas's arm, made her way to Eileen's other side, and looked back-and-forth from Eileen to Alfred with all the wonder she could put into her expression.

"The old castle hae dungeons, Alfred? How fascinating!

Will ye shew us?"

Alfred looked to Eileen.

Kelsey looked at her new friend too.

Eileen grinned at Kelsey with a look that clearly said "Thank ye" before she turned her huge charming smile back onto Alfred.

"Och, would ye?"

Alfred looked at the other men.

Tavish shrugged at him.

Seumas looked at Kelsey with a question in his eyes much like the one Alfred had asked Eileen.

Kelsey made herself maintain eye contact with Seumas and not look over at Tavish. The red-haired man was good-looking enough that it wasn't difficult. He seemed nice enough. But she'd only just met him. Still, she and Tavish needed to get into the underground castle. She felt the lie in her smile even as she gave it to him.

Seumas clapped his brother on the back.

"Aye, let us gae and tell Maw we shall be a while longer."

Eileen elbowed Kelsey in the ribs just then.

Kelsey broke into laughter when she saw the look Eileen gave her, which bordered between "Woo woo!" and "I thought so!" And then Kelsey did look at Tavish to see his reaction to this whole little exchange.

He moved up to the front of the group, opened a door, and went inside without looking back at her.

Alfred took the rest of them through the same door.

"Maw!"

"Maw!"

"Maw!"

"Maw!"

Eileen's four children ran over and all found a way to hug her at the same time.

Thus encumbered, Eileen still found a way to sort of curtsy at Alfred and Seumas's mother, a woman of about 50 who looked kind but clever.

"I thank ye sae much, ma'am. I hope they were na tae much trouble."

Alfred stepped over.

"Maw, I'm verra happy for ye tae meet Eileen. Eileen, this is my maw, Isabel."

Isabel looked back-and-forth between Alfred and Eileen with a calmly controlled joy. And then she put her hands on the children and patted them gently and smiled at them when their little eyes looked up at hers.

"It was nay trouble at all, dear."

Alfred held out his arm for Eileen.

"Och good. Then ye will na mind at all watching them for a little while longer while Tavish, Seumas, and I give Eileen and her new apprentice Kelsey a tour o the dungeons."

On hearing this, Eileen's children piped up.

"The dungeons!"

"We want to go to the dungeons tae!"

"Och!"

"Maw, can we?"

Eileen opened her mouth to say something, but Isabel knelt down and held out her arms.

"Nah nah, the dungeons aren't any place for children. Come on ower tae auntie Isabel. I'll tak ye doon tae the kitchen and see if Sorcha has anything sweet we can mak for ye."

The children rushed over to Isabel and let her hug

them while Eileen walked over and took Alfred's arm, and then the two led the rest of them out of the nursery, down the corridor, down the stairs, and out through the kitchen. Just before they left the Castle, they picked up torches from a bin and lighted them in the fireplace.

There were lamps burning in all the taverns, but the vendor carts were gone for the night, and only a few people wandered the streets—most of them obviously drunk, walking arm in arm.

The whole way to the underground castle entrance, Seumas walked by Kelsey's side. He was a perfect gentleman, never taking any liberties, but he did catch her by the arm once when she stumbled, preventing her from a nasty fall.

His attention made her self-conscious about wanting to stare at the starry sky. She did catch glimpses of the stars now and then, and there were far more than she ever knew existed. She could even see galaxies, and of course the Milky Way.

She did her best not to sigh, not to give away that she was in no way interested. Encouraging Seumas had seemed a good idea at the time, so now she needed to sleep in the bed she had made—hopefully just figuratively.

Every so often, she tried to catch Tavish's eye. If she was honest with herself, she would admit she wanted reassurance that she was not alone here, that someone else understood how it felt to be 700 years outside one's own time. But he was walking on the other side of Seumas and was never looking at her at the same time she was looking at him.

And then they were at this different underground castle entrance, where an elaborate trap door stood open, revealing a narrow stone staircase going down into blackness. It was much farther back from the cliffs than the ruined tower house which covered those three trapdoors in her time. She cast about for some landmarks, thinking to try and dig up this new trap door in her time.

Once she thought she had it triangulated so that she could find it again, she tried again to make eye contact with Tavish. But again he was looking instead somewhere else. She kept looking at him as long as seemed possible without it getting awkward, but he still didn't happen to look at her.

Two kilted guards armed with claymores stood there on watch, but they nodded to Alfred as he approached.

"Evening, Sir."

"Evening Dubh, Luthais," he said to them, "Seumas and Tavish and I wull be taking these ladies doon tae the docks for a quick look."

Dubh and Luthais bowed their heads toward him.

"Verra well, Sir."

Alfred and Eileen went down the stairs first single file, holding the wall with one hand and their torches high with the other. At the same time, Seumas and Tavish both gestured in front of them for Kelsey to follow so that they could take up the rear.

Kelsey held up her torch and followed Eileen down the stairs.

It had been dark when she and Tavish left here this morning, but their eyes had been adjusted to the darkness, and they had been coming out toward the light of the sun. Now they were going down into the darkness—and it seemed foreboding indeed. Thankfully, she wasn't the only one who thought so, or she would've felt really alone.

Eileen brought it up first, smiling at Alfred in the torchlight.

"Are ye sure 'tis safe down here? 'Tis dreadfully dark."

Alfred chuckled.

"Do ye hae second thoughts on coming doon to the dungeons, lass?"

Oh no. Before he had a chance to talk Eileen out of exploring the dungeons, Kelsey butted in.

"I know I'm havin second an e'en third thoughts aboot comin doon here, but with three strong warriors tae protect us, I know we will be fine. Aye, Eileen?"

Eileen gave Kelsey that same impish grin. And she leaned into Alfred as they all started to walk side-by-side along the corridor—which meant Seumas came up beside Kelsey and Tavish stayed by himself in the back. And Eileen winked at her before she turned to Alfred and all but batted her eyelashes.

"Dinna leave my side, and all my thoughts will stay in order."

Alfred put his arm around Eileen's waist and turned to address everyone.

"This is where the odd parts o the corridor start." He turned toward the wall and pointed to some Celtic runes that Kelsey could see announced a secret door. "Ivry sae often along the corridor, ye wull see these same runes. We dinna know what they mean. Several o us hae theories." He raised his eyebrow and invited speculation.

Here, at last, Tavish met eyes with Kelsey. He raised his own eyebrow, and she knew without a shadow of a doubt what he was asking: "Is it another secret door?"

Kelsey nodded the ever slightest to him.

He pressed his lips together and looked around, and

118

again she knew exactly what he was saying to her, they'd known each other so well: "Be ready to come back here and explore it. I'm going to cause a distraction at the first opportunity I see."

She made the tiniest nod to him again.

Meanwhile, Eileen was gushing with enthusiasm at Alfred.

"Och, I hae heard stories aboot the things doon in these caves! The ancient druids used tae dae ritual sacrifices doon here they say! There's supposit tae be aw kinds o secret passageways gang deep intae the cliffs! An aw sorts o secret rooms with treasure inside! Och, and dungeons as well—ye know, where they did thaes sacrifices!"

Alfred gave her an amused smile and humored her a bit.

"Forsooth, all I hae seen are these strange Celtic markings. I dinna doubt the Celts livit in these caves long ago. As for the rest, yer guess is as guid as mine." He bowed his head to Eileen a bit, and she caressed his cheek. "Come, we must get on with the tour doon tae the dungeons if we are tae get tae bed afore the cock crows."

Instead of letting Seumas accompany Kelsey as he had before, Tavish fell in next to Seumas and clapped a hand on his back and spoke to him uproariously, demanding all the man's attention as they walked down the corridor.

"I'll wager we find altars in the dungeons gin we look well enough. Whit say ye?"

Seumas was taken in.

"Och I'll willingly take yer money! We hae been doon thare hundrits o times on the watches, and hae seen nay sign o an altar…"

Kelsey knew this was Tavish giving her an opportunity to explore the secret door, so she wasted no time slipping away to go back and get it open.

It opened to a stairway going down. She held her torch down as far she could in front of her, but when that only revealed more stairs and more darkness, she went ahead and started going down, although not as fast as she might have were there light in the room. Praying that she wouldn't stumble and fall and break her nose on the hard stone floor, she at last came to the bottom of the stairs and into a room. It was full of stuff, but rather than take the time to notice just what it was, she quickly powered up her camera and took several photos, then put it on screensaver and stuck it back in the pouch in the side of her leather backpack so she could rush back up the stairs, close the door, and run to hopefully catch up with the others before they noticed she was gone.

No such luck.

But to her amusement, it was Tavish who called out to her. She hoped only she could tell he was faking his anger.

"Where did ye go, Kelsey? Ye shouldn't go away from the group like thon!"

Inspiration struck, and Kelsey put her hand on her abdomen.

"Och, I have na gone anywhere, it's just that I have a wee stitch in my side. I canna gae as fast as ye can. Gae on ahead o me. I'll make ma way at ma own pace. Surely thare canna be any danger in here, with the guards at both ends o the corridor."

Seumas moved forward as if to help her, but Tavish held him back, still speaking as if he were angry, but unseen, he was smiling at her.

"Nay, Kelsey. Gae back and wait for us with the guards at the entrance, if ye canna keep up."

Seumas took in a breath as if to make a case for Kelsey to come along with them.

But Tavish turned a genuinely angry look on him, and Seumas backed down.

Kelsey waved at them all and turned back to go the way she had come, saying farewell to them over her shoulder.

"Verra well. See ye at the top."

Just before she turned around, she caught an apologetic look from Seumas and shook her head no, hoping he would let it drop.

He seemed to, because she heard them all going off the other way down the corridor behind her.

She kept on going a little ways, until she only heard them faintly and knew they'd gone around the corner. And then she went back and opened the second secret doorway. She took pictures in there with two fingers showing on her hand, so that later on when she looked at the pictures, she would know where this stuff was.

She catalogued a dozen more rooms this way. Unlike the second door room, most of them were very old bedrooms. None had any dust, because of the sophisticated yet simple air circulation system which permeated the place.

The whole time, she kept her eye out for any sign of Brian, but the only thing she noticed was that one of the beds looked slept in. She made a mental note of which room that was before she moved on.

But then the thirteenth door she came to led to a passageway that went down several flights of stairs and around corners and down long hallways—until the last secret door she opened dropped her off in the rough cave near the docks.

Sure enough, bows and quivers of arrows hung from the grooves in the walls. Tavish had been right about those grooves, and no wonder. But that didn't bother her nearly as much as the fact that she had noisily emerged out of the wall on her hands and knees, right behind Seumas.

Aon deug

Kelsey met Tavish's eyes, and in just a moment, with only the slightest facial expressions, they held a lengthy silent conversation.

"Hm! I'm impressed that you found your way back to us through the walls!"

"Believe me, I am too."

"Did you find the artifact?"

"No, and I really looked hard, covering as much ground as I could."

"It's okay, I'll just keep giving you opportunities to look."

"Understood. And anyway, I'm having fun looking."

"This is serious business, Kelsey—"

"Of course it is. Quick, do something about Seumas!"

She saw Tavish cast his glance about then, but it was too late.

Seumas turned around and made his way to her side protectively, narrowing his eyes at Tavish, who wrinkled his brow a little and playfully smirked at Kelsey while the large redheaded man lingered between them and extended his hand to her, offering to help her up.

"Kelsey! Verra glad I am to see ye made it back tae us." He gave Tavish a sidelong glance. "Did ye stumble, Kelsey? Please, allow me tae help ye up."

But she looked to Tavish.

Seumas got out of his way.

And Tavish came forward and tenderly helped her up. After he did, it was clear that he got just as much of a thrill holding her hand and she did his, because he lingered there, looking into her eyes and giving the back of her hand the barest caress with his fingers.

Alfred was standing there in the group with them, holding Eileen by the waist, and he cleared his throat.

"The dungeons we promisit tae show ye are around this last bend, on the other side o the docks."

Kelsey caught an 'I told you so' raise of Eileen's eyebrows, along with a warm smile of congratulations. She returned the look in kind, and Eileen's smile changed to one of joy.

Tavish hung back with Kelsey a bit and gestured for the others to go in front of them.

"You go on ahead. We wull be there shortly."

Seumas and Alfred took the hint and started off, but Eileen looked over her shoulder as they left and winked at Kelsey.

But just when they started walking that way, they heard

shouts from the docks.

"Boats!"

"They're coming!"

"Get the bows!"

"The MacDonalds are attacking!"

Tavish and Seumas and Alfred didn't hesitate to grab bows and quivers from the wall and rush down to the docks, putting the quivers on their backs and drawing an arrow each while they ran.

Kelsey and Eileen stood there staring at each other, blinking.

Eileen swallowed.

"Dae ye think we shoud tak bows ower an gae help them?"

Kelsey grimaced.

"Dae ye know how tae use a bow? Because I don't."

Eileen shook her head.

"Nay, I dinna either."

Meanwhile, they could hear the shouts of battle coming from the end of the hallway around the corner.

Alfred was giving orders.

"Warwick, tak the boat on the left. Seumas, tak the neist boat tae the richt o Warwick's. Ian, the boat tae the richt o Seumas's..."

The other men were saying "Aye," accompanied by a lot of scuffling about, and in the distance, the MacDonalds were shouting their own orders, which the women could hear, but not really understand because of the general noise of the sea between them.

Kelsey quietly took a bow and a quiver down anyway, put the quiver on over her leather backpack, then crept over to the wall between her and the battle. She looked back to see if Eileen was going to do the same, and then waited for her.

When Eileen caught up to her, the sounds of the battle were lower and the waves breaking against the rocks seemed louder.

Eileen whispered, "Ye are na charging in there, are ye?"

Kelsey crept forward along the wall till she was almost at the bend, then turned her head back toward Eileen and waited again for her to catch up before she whispered back.

"Nay, but I am no gaun'ae juist stand around here without knowing what's gang on ower thare."

Eileen nodded vigorously and urged Kelsey on with a tap on the waist with the back of her hand.

Kelsey crept along the wall until she could peek around the bend, holding her torch behind her so that its light didn't give away her location.

Tavish, Alfred, Seumas, and the other dock defenders had thrown their torches down on the smooth stone floor of the dock area and found cover behind various rocks, where they were busy shooting one arrow after another into the dozens of men who were approaching on half a dozen lantern lit boats. Most of these men were rowing, but a few had bows out and were shooting back.

Eileen started to come around the corner by Kelsey's side with her torch held high, but Kelsey frantically grabbed her skirt and held her back.

Tavish met Kelsey's eyes full of fear for her, nodding urgently back toward the secret door she had just come from, silently pleading for her to please go to safety.

The moment she had waited seven years for had finally come. She saw such deep love and caring in his eyes that her heart commanded her to run to him and fall into his arms and never let go. But her head knew he had to pay attention to the battle and would only worry needlessly about her if she stuck around.

She struggled with this choice for a moment, but then another enemy arrow whizzed by and she came to her senses. Putting as much love and caring as she possibly could in her own eyes, she nodded at Tavish, then turned around and gently took Eileen by the elbows to keep her from going into the battle scene.

"There are arrows flying all places, Eileen. We canna gae oot thare."

Eileen struggled with her.

"But we canna make it back tae the top before the invaders reach us. I'd rather dee oot thare shootin at them than feel them at ma back as I run away!"

Kelsey shook her head quickly.

"We can gae up unseen. I found a way. Come on!"

Eileen looked doubtful, but she quit struggling and followed Kelsey over to the secret door, which was down low to the floor.

Kelsey put her bow down on top of Eileen's, handed Eileen her torch, and then wasted no time opening the secret door. With the invader's cries getting louder and the sound of feet scrambling on the rocks ringing through the cave, the two of them got themselves, the torches, and the bows inside, and then Kelsey hurried to close the secret door again.

She and Eileen held each other for a moment and cringed, listening, but determination overtook Kelsey, and she withdrew from Eileen, slung her bow over her shoulder, picked up her torch, and started to climb the stairs—careful to hold up her long skirts with her other hand.

"Come on, let's go get help!"

Hope bloomed on Eileen's face then, and the weaver eagerly climbed the stairs as well.

The two women ran all the way up, went through the other secret door, and then ran up the passageway and the final stairs to the entrance guards before they all but fell on the ground, exhausted and gasping for breath while they explained.

"Dubh! Luthais! We're under attack!"

"Please! Send more men down there!"

"Dozens o invaders are coming by boat!"

"The guards are holding them off with arrows for now, but hurry!"

Dubh and Luthais blew on the ram's horns they had around their necks, and a runner came over and left.

A few moments later, Laird Malcomb led over dozens of kilted warriors who Kelsey recognized from supper in the castle a few hours before. They all went running down the stairs single file with their claymores strapped to their backs. Up on the sea-facing battlements, dozens more guards were rolling huge stones into the water below. Some yielded distant splashes, and others scored the satisfying sound of a boat's floor cracking and enemy voices calling out in alarm.

Kelsey tried to get up to follow Laird Malcomb downstairs, but she had used up all her adrenaline. Her shaking legs wouldn't cooperate. She looked over at Eileen, who wasn't doing any better.

She'd sat there gasping for breath for a minute, trying to get her legs under her, when she felt a gentle hand on her back and turned to see the sympathetic face of Isabel, Alfred and Seumas's mother.

"I am indebtit tae ye, Kelsey and Eileen, for coming in such earnest tae get help for my sons—even if, God forbid, they should perish." She stood and extended a hand to each of them. "Come inside and let us await them together."

Eileen's children ran to greet their mother before she got halfway down the hallway to the nursery.

"Maw!"

"Maw!"

"Maw!"

"Maw!"

Once more, the small blonde woman was enveloped by her four small blond children, who hugged her various arms and legs and waist.

Kelsey and Isabel stayed back and enjoyed this scene, which while chaotic in itself was calming in contrast to the battle outside. But the battle soon intruded. Even within the thick walls of the castle fortress, they could hear the muffled voice of the captain of the guard shouting orders outside.

Isabel took Kelsey's hand and made her way over to Eileen and the children.

"Let us crowd around the small windae i the nursery an see whit we can see, eh?"

Eileen nodded and led the way.

"Come, children."

Kelsey and Eileen put their bows down on the table and took off their quivers and set them beside the bows.

They all crowded into the narrow arrow-slit window. Unable to move around, Kelsey's view was limited to one section of the battlement, but it was satisfying to watch the kilted warriors there pushing their stones over the edge at the enemy boats. Eileen had a view of the soldiers rolling the stones up a ramp onto the battlement, and from time to time she would comment on that. Isabel had commanded the view of the exit from the downstairs, and she watched it silently, her face a mixture of fear and hope for her sons. All the children could see was the night sky full of billions of stars, and the women took turns picking the children up now and again so they could see what the women were talking about.

Kelsey's breath caught.

"They're all rushing tae ma section o the battlement!"

She was jostled as everyone tried to see what she was talking about. One of the kids managed to get in there and take her place.

"Look! They are! Everyone's running ower thare."

Kelsey looked at Eileen who gently pulled the child out of the way—but then Eileen herself pushed into that spot so she could see.

"This has tae mean all the boats are tryin tae dock! Get them! Get them!"

All the children joined in with their mother, yelling and screaming as if the people out there across the courtyard could hear them, and as if they would work more frantically if they did.

"Get them! Get them!"

It reminded Kelsey of the football games her parents used to attend with her at her high school. She nosed in there, pushing Eileen's face away so she could see.

Dà dheug

The boats were coming in to land now, and Tavish's fellow guards were rushing them, so he could no longer use his bow. He set it aside and drew his Claymore off his back.

The Rocky dock area echoed with the metal on metal ringing sounds of sword fighting—and then the stones started to fall from the cliffs above.

Whoosh! Foom! Crack!

Tavish and Seumas and all their fellow guards cheered.

An answering cheer came from above—along with more of those blessed stones which were tearing the boats to shreds and even hitting a few of the attackers directly.

But there were so many enemies. They abandoned their boats and swam for the rocky shoreline, climbing over each other in their enthusiasm to raid this ancient castle.

Tavish rushed in with the other defending guards, and then he was fighting for his life—hacking and slashing his way through the bodies that scrambled up on the rocks, dodging and ducking the swords that came at him.

It went on and on and on, until he could feel himself tiring.

But all he could think about the whole time he fought the intruders was surviving long enough to get back to Kelsey so he could get her home. Why had he brought her here? The old time was far more dangerous that anything they would do to her in the new time! Yes, he'd known she'd love it here in the old time, and he'd been wishing for years that he could share this with her, but it had been selfish and stupid of him to bring her here. What was he thinking?

Well, done was done. All he could do now was survive this so that he could get back to her—and get her home safely.

They had the high ground, up on the rocks while the enemy tried to climb up from the sea. But they were outnumbered six to one, and Tavish was just about too tired to go on fighting when he heard the battle cry of more fellow guards coming down the inner hallway through the castle toward him. His fellow guards out here on the dock heard it too, and they all let out a cheer.

This reenergized him just enough—he hoped—so that

the reinforcements would get here and he wouldn't die and leave Kelsey abandoned.

His fellow guards were almost at the docks, and he was getting ready to retreat and let them take over, when he felt a blow to the back of his head and the world went dark and quiet.

Trì deug

Kelsey, Eileen, Isabel, and all the children were cheering. All the men on the battlements had come down to the entrance to the underground castle, and the men were running out, slapping the hands of their fellow guards, not unlike sports teams did the beginning of games. They cheered even louder when they saw Seumas come out, and then again when they saw Alfred come out.

A few moments after that, Eileen and Isabel ran out the door together, presumably to go greet Isabel's victorious sons together.

The children stayed with Kelsey.

"Where's yer friend?"

"Did he gae doon thare with Alfred and Seumas?"

Kelsey didn't look at them, just kept staring out the window, telling herself he would come out in any moment. He would be the next one. No, the next one. No, the one after that. The next one now.

"Aye, he shall be coming oot any moment now," she said.

The eldest child scolded her younger brothers and sister.

"Hush, ye dafties! She's afraid he's dead and wull na be able tae come oot!"

Kelsey winced at that, but she didn't dare look the little girl in the eye or say anything to her. Kelsey knew that would break the dam and let out the tears of despair that she was only barely holding in. She took a deep calming breath, telling herself there was no way she was going to be crying when Tavish came up, all triumphant after his battle.

And then she heard everyone else's voices from far down the hallway and knew the awful truth. Alfred's voice was the loudest.

"We thought he came up here before we did. Are ye sure he isna up here with Kelsey?"

Eileen spoke in hushed tones when she answered him.

"Aye, we are sure. We left her alone up here with the children when we came down tae greet ye."

Seumas spoke up.

"Och, there are several ways tae come up. Mayhap he came up another way and is sitting with Kelsey even now. The two o them seemed very friendly with each other just before the battle started."

Isabel spoke to them softly.

"Hush nae. Let us pray we find him with her, but if we dae na, she will be verra distraught, sae dinna vex her."

The children once more ran to their mother when the group came in, but this time she hadn't been gone long enough for them to cling to her and yell out. It was late, and the excitement was over, and they were starting to show their sleepiness.

"Can we go home now, Maw?"

"I'm tired."

"Aye, isna it after our bedtime?"

Eileen laughed softly at the children's precociousness, but she ended it quickly, glancing over at her new friend.

"Aye, that it is. Alfred, can we take ye up now on that offer tae see us home? Kelsey, as I said before, ye are more than welcome tae come along."

Kelsey looked over at Isabel.

"If it doesna fash ye ower much, I wish tae stay here till…"

Isabel came over quickly and put her arms around Kelsey.

"Nay, it doesna fash me at all. Ye are welcome tae stay. Come, let us gae doon tae the kitchen an hae some tea an scones while we wait for young Tavish tae come up." She nodded her head toward the door while looking at the others. "Alfred, gae on and see Eileen and the children home. Seamus, gae see if ye can find yer friend Tavish. Mayhap he's hit his head or some such and needs yer help."

The others all took the hint and shuffled out of the room. Not even the children said anything.

Kelsey didn't dare look up at them, though. The looks of pity she knew she would see on their faces would be just too unbearable. She sniffed and blinked the tears away as Isabel rocked her gently back and forth in her arms. And then she looked at Isabel with all the pleading she could will into her eyes and spoke to her through her sobs as she stood up, bringing the older woman up with her.

"Please, let us gae doon thare an speak tae some o the guard. What if Seamus misses Tavish lyin injurit and needing some men tae carry him up!"

Isabel nodded and kept her arm around Kelsey, leading her to the door of the nursery.

"Aye. That we shall do." The motherly woman kept murmuring affirmations of Kelsey's idea as they went down the hall, through the huge kitchen, and out into the Castle yard entrance to the dungeons. "Aye, there's a good idea, lass. Aye, we shall send some guards back doon the other way from where Seamus goes."

When they finally got to the guards, it had started to rain. Kelsey couldn't wait for Isabel to get around to telling them what needed to be done. The only thing she could think to be thankful for was the fact that she was able to steel herself and speak without sobbing.

"Dubh! Luthais! Tavish is still doon thare! He hasna come up! I am sure he's doon thare bleeding somewhere. Please, let me gae doon tae find him!" Without waiting for an answer, she was already pushing her way through them.

But Isabel stopped her with a gentle but firm grab of her arm.

"Kelsey, ye must stay up here with me, lass. Ye are tae tyrit."

Suddenly Kelsey did feel tired once more, and she all but collapsed into Isabel's arms. She looked up at the guards with her pleading eyes.

"Please, please send doon tae find him."

Isabel held Kelsey and undid the brooch that fastened her thick plaid erasaid to her overdress so that she could put it over both of them to keep the rain off while she spoke to one of the guards.

"Aye, dae send some men doon, Dubh." And then the older woman turned back toward the kitchen, gently tugging Kelsey along with her under the thick plaid. "Come, lass. Let us get in oot o the wet. The men will search. Ye hae done well seeing tae it."

Just before they went in the kitchen door, Kelsey turned around to make sure Dubh was sending a search party. Only when she was satisfied to see him speaking to a squadron of guards did she allow Seumas's mom to tug her inside.

Isabel parked Kelsey in a comfy chair by the fireplace. In a remarkable show of consideration, she turned the chair toward the kitchen door and propped the door open so that Kelsey could see through the rain to the underground castle entrance from where she sat.

"Just ye rest there nae, lass. Naught can happen but that ye shull see from here, ye ken? I wull brew us a nice pot o tea, eh?" She dipped a copper kettle in a large vat of water and then leaned over Kelsey to place it right on top of the hot coals that had been banked to keep the fire lit overnight.

Kelsey tried to get up.

"I'm far tae worried aboot Tavish tae just sit here and watch ye work. Let me help ye."

But Isabel put a firm hand on Kelsey's shoulder and held her down in the chair.

"Nay, nay." She gently raised Kelsey's chin until their eyes met. "An honor it is tae serve ye, Kelsey. Did ye think I didna mean it when I said I owed ye a debt for getting help in time tae save my sons?"

Kelsey relaxed back in the chair and gave Isabel an embarrassed and grudging smile.

"Dinna think o it, Isabel. If I'm tae be truthful, I did na dae it for yer sons at all. I was only thinking o Tavish."

Admitting this brought the tears to Kelsey's eyes again, and she broke down into a series of sobs, with Isabel patting her shoulder and holding her hand, and finally hugging her tight until her sobs wore themselves out.

Isabel made the tea and poured it into two pretty earthenware mugs, got out a matching earthenware plate, then winked at Kelsey and revealed where the scones were hidden, probably from the children, under a bunch of folded cleaning cloths. She sat down on the hearth and put the mugs and the scones there too, then took one of Kelsey's hands in hers and bowed her head.

"Laird God, we pray for Kelsey's dear friend Tavish. We fear we have lost sight o him. Howsoever, Ye dae know where he is. Wherever thon may be, please tak care o him for us until we meet him again." She squeezed Kelsey's hand. "Amen."

"Amen."

Kelsey smiled her thanks at Isabel and resisted the urge to throw herself into the woman's arms again and hold close to the only person who was any comfort. Her mind wanted to go off into a panic about what she would do if she didn't find Tavish again—if he...

But no. She would not allow herself to think about that.

Making herself believe that the men would find Tavish only slightly injured somewhere and bring him up again to her, Kelsey took a big bite of her scone and washed it down with half her cup of tea, all while staring intently out the open door at the empty entrance where she hoped he would come out any minute.

Huddling inside their tiny guard shack out of the rain, Dubh and Luthais grimly waved at her every few minutes, and she halfheartedly waved back.

The silence became oppressive though, so Kelsey made small talk with Isabel.

"Mmmm, this is guid tea. It's no a kynd I hae tastit before. Whit is it?"

Isabel took a dainty sip of her own tea.

"Och, I hopit ye would like it. Alfred and Seumas say it tastes like soap, heh! Juist some flowers thon grow oot i the meadow. Sorcha has a name for thaim, but I can't bring it tae mind right now. Dae ye like her scones?"

Kelsey had just taken another big bite of her scone. She chewed quickly and washed it down with the rest of her tea.

"Och, aye. And I dae think I taste… Can it be dates in them?"

Isabel slumped on her perch on the hearth.

"Aye, dates they are! Och, I was gaun'ae have ye guess what they were. Wherever did ye hae dates before—and dae ye know how far they come from!"

Kelsey was starting to feel at home with this woman who was being so kind to her—in fact, sitting there by the fire all toasty, she had a warm fuzzy feeling all over—so she didn't really think about what she said next, beyond what it took to say it in Gaelic.

"Ma maw loves dates. She puts thaim in all things. Aye, they're a little dear, coming all the way from Arabia, but Da does na mind because they mak her sae happy."

Isabel sat up and took notice.

"My, yer da must be well off, tae afford sae many dates. How did he make his fortune?"

Kelsey continued to watch out the door for Tavish's return, but she felt grateful to Isabel for the company while she did so, and didn't want the motherly woman to leave. Alfred was likely back by now from walking Eileen home. Ack, here was hoping he didn't come in the kitchen. She felt way too tired for company right now.

"Aye, Eileen askit aboot thon earlier, and forsooth 'tis quite a tale. My da is an excellent salesman. A merchant has attachit him, and he follows this merchant all ower the world, wheelin and dealin for him."

Isabel looked even more impressed.

"Och, A had na idea! Sae yer da has been tae Arabia, then, and likely tae China and all!"

Kelsey nodded.

"Aye, he has."

Isabel gathered up the dishes and washed them with one of the cleaning rags and some water from the vat.

"Sae that's where ye get yer uncanny knowledge o sums, then, aye?"

Kelsey chuckled.

"Aye, I suppose it is."

Isabel was drying the dishes and putting them back up on the board.

"I imagine yer da has telt ye some amazin stories from his travels."

Sleepiness was taking Kelsey over, and it was a pleasant feeling. The comfy chair was just large enough for her to lean to the side and draw her knees up so that she could rest in a fetal position.

"Och, aye. One time he brought home kimonos for Maw and me, from Japan..."

Kelsey giggled one note at how funny this story was,

and she really wanted to share it with Isabel, but it just seemed like too much effort. She closed her eyes for a moment, and then she was vaguely aware of something soft and warm being placed over the side of her away from the fire. And then she nestled into sweet nothingness.

Ceithir deug

Tavish woke up in a pitch black room, sore in every part of his body and with a pounding headache, lying in a strange bed. Where the hell was he? It was no place he'd been before, that was for sure.

The bed was almost too soft. And it was deep, so that he was lying on his side and only his top arm could reach out of the bed, which was more like a bowl full of blankets than a modern mattress bed. He'd had a friend in high school whose parents had a waterbed, and that was about as close to this as he'd ever heard of before.

He stretched out his top arm, looking for the edge of the bowl so that he could pull himself out. When he found the edge, he froze. The bowl was made of stone! Wanting to get out his flashlight, he reached down to where his sporran should have been—but didn't feel it. Maybe it had twisted around on his body. He maneuvered around inside the blankets, patting all around his hips and waist area, but didn't find it.

A surge of adrenaline rushed through his blood, but the only things he had to fight over the pouch and his belt were these blankets. He was wondering if it would be easier to struggle around inside the blankets to search the bowl, or if he should instead pull himself out of the bowl and dig the blankets out in his search—when he heard an unfamiliar man's voice and saw candlelight dancing on the carved rock ceiling of what could only be one of the dungeons in the underground castle.

"Are ye looking for this, lad?"

Tavish yanked himself up and out of the bowl of a bed and was on his feet in seconds, reaching over his shoulder for his sword. When it wasn't there either, he lowered his arms and studied the other man warily. Dressed in white robes and wearing his beard long, this man definitely had that evil wizard thing going on. In one hand he held up a candle, and in the other, Tavish's sporran.

Tavish reached for it.

"Aye."

His mind had nicknamed this old man Saruman, and he was surprised when he let him have it. He put it on and felt inside. So far as he could recall, all his belongings were in there. All except one.

"What about my sword. Where is that?"

Saruman put a sad look in his eyes and shook his head.

"Nay, thare wis na sword on ye when I found ye

146

knockit oot among the dead oot thare at the docks."

Tavish looked around for the door out of the room, but didn't see it. There had to be a door. Saruman had come through it with his candle just a moment ago.

"Och, well. I can get another sword in the castle armory. I thank ye for the... rest an all, but I must be gang back up tae the castle now. Will ye show me the way?"

But Saruman took his hand out of one of the pockets of his snowy white robes, opened it up under his mouth, and blew some kind of dust all over Tavish, who sneezed three times before collapsing into the bowl bed once more. This elderly man couldn't really be an evil wizard, could he?

Through the growing haziness of his mind, Tavish searched Saruman's face.

"Why?"

The man moved forward and covered Tavish up with some of the blankets. Tavish tried to reach out and grab the man's hand, but found that he couldn't even move. He was out before the man answered him.

***

But Kelsey appeared in Tavish's dreams.

Instead of Gehrig's wife's long plaid dress, she was wearing the clothes he'd seen her in the most often: her Highlands costume from his parents' Renaissance faire. Only in his dream, her long brown hair hung down, and she was wearing makeup.

"Tavish! You're alive! Oh, thank God! Where are you?"

This sure was an odd dream. Oh well. Might as well answer her.

"Uh, I'm in a weird rock bowl bed in one of the rooms in the underground castle, and there's this Saruman dude who just blew something in my face that made me go to sleep."

As he said this, he appeared in the bowl-shaped bed in his dream, too.

Kelsey came over to the side of his bed and frantically looked him all over.

"Are you okay?"

Having her this close with her eyes all over him wasn't good for his concentration. Forgetting how odd a dream this was, he pulled her into the bed with him. Suddenly, they were both naked. And the dream got really good. Who knew a bowl-shaped bed could be so useful? This allowed him to relax and really enjoy her company afterward, while they lay there in each other's arms.

"I've really missed you, Kel."

She pulled away just enough to look him in the eyes, and her eyes were full of pain, and brand-new tears.

"Then why did you drop out of my life?"

Guilt and pain assaulted his psyche on one side, anger and frustration on the other. He couldn't stand it. He pulled her close to him and held her tight—truth be told more for himself than for her. He couldn't hold her close enough.

"Please don't be mad at me, Kel. I want to tell you, believe me I do. Believe me when I say I can't. It's not something I can choose to do. I literally can't tell you."

Hurt came into her voice, but she didn't pull away from him. If anything, she held him tighter.

"We were so close, Tavish. I mean, I thought we were. I thought I knew everything about you. And you were never like this back then. Can you tell me what happened at least?"

He stroked her hair.

"I didn't know back then, Kel. I didn't know..." He tried to tell her, but the words just would not come out of his mouth, not even in a dream. Whenever that happened, he kept trying to speak to her about it until he found words he could say. "And the moment my parents told me about it, I took myself out of your life. You deserve to find someone else and have children who won't be bound by... some promise one of my ancestors made centuries ago."

She must've found it easier to talk this way too, because she just stayed there in his arms and let him caress her, instead of pulling away and looking him in the eye again.

"Well at least I know you don't hate me. That's actually a really sweet reason for you to have left, and I'm glad I know. But Tavish, you should have had enough faith in me to let me decide if I wanted you bad enough to put up with this curse."

He laid his head against hers, willing his thoughts, his love, his very being to radiate into hers somehow so that she could feel it.

"Yeah. I should have."

Oddly, now she did break away and look him in the eye. As much as she could break away in a bowl bed, anyway.

"You know what?"

She looked so excited and enthusiastic he couldn't help teasing her a little.

"No, what?"

She scrunched her nose at him in that adorable way she had.

"It's kind of a good thing you shut me out for those seven years—but not for the reasons you think.

Remember when you came back from getting me those clothes, and you thought I'd been invisible?"

He got his elbows under him and sort of sat up to face her.

"Yeah. That was even weirder than this dream."

She paused briefly, and then laughed a little.

"Well I didn't lie to you. You really were invisible to me, too—after Brian the Druid went away."

"Brian the Druid?"

"Yeah, Brian the Druid. That's probably who the Saruman dude is, the one who made you go to sleep. Anyway, he took one look at my ring and decided I was a druid too. He called me Priestess."

"O… K… I don't really see how that makes it a good thing that I had to fade out of your life seven years ago."

"Don't you see? If I'm a druid too, then maybe I can learn to remove your curse!"

She just disappeared then, as if she was a character in a video game and her player had logged out.

His dreams were unremarkable after that, boring and forgettable, but the next thing he knew, he heard Kelsey's voice in his ear at barely a whisper, and it wasn't a dream. She was also leaning her hand on his chest, shaking him a bit. He felt her breath in his ear, warm and intimate.

"Tavish, wake up. Tavish, wake up. Wake up, Tavish."

He opened his eyes.

There she was, even sexier in reality than she'd been in his dream. The light he could see by was coming from her flashlight, which she had trained on the floor of the cave room as she knelt by his bedside. Her face was very close.

Before he remembered what had happened between them was just a dream, he reached out and pulled her to him and kissed her, putting all his need for her into it, all the longing he had felt over the past seven years.

She returned the kiss—and to his surprise, she did so without hesitation.

He deepened the kiss, inspired by the mood that had been set in his dream.

She returned the deepened kiss for a moment, but before he could pull her into the bed with him and make last night's dream a reality, she pulled away slightly and took a deep breath, then spoke softly, her warm brown eyes entreating him even as she grabbed his arm and started pulling him up.

"We have to get out of here. Please get up."

He gently took the hands that she'd put on his arm and waited for her to meet his eyes again.

"Wait. How did you find me?"

She gave him one last intense moment of intimacy from her eyes, and then she helped him get up out of the bed bowl while she answered him in her soft feminine voice.

"I was in this room yesterday while I was looking for the artifact while you distracted our friends…" She pressed her lips together and swallowed. "And then I recognized it when I saw you in your dream."

Adrenaline surged through him on hearing that, and he recognized the fear he felt. But it gradually faded. He hadn't told her, and he certainly didn't want to fight her, nor run from her. All he really wanted to do was pull her into the bed with him, but now he had woken up enough to remember it wasn't safe here. He let her help him out of bed.

She turned around and went over to a spot on the wall

and messed with it until she opened one of those secret doors, then turned her head back toward him.

"Come on, before Brian the Druid catches up with us!"

He followed her through the secret door and into the stone corridor, then kept looking both ways down the corridor while she closed the secret door.

"No sign of him so far."

She got up and motioned for him to follow her, and they ran up the corridor toward the exit, speaking in hushed voices between deep breaths.

"Good. I guess he got your sword?"

"He says my sword wasn't on me when he found me."

"Do you believe him?"

"I'm not sure."

"Yeah, I'm not sure if we can trust him either."

Tavish grabbed her hand as they ran and squeezed it. She squeezed back, so he tenderly kept hold of the small part of her he could have. Not knowing was killing him though.

"So. Do you remember the rest of the dream?"

They were getting close to the exit. They could finally see the guards up there, now that they'd rounded the final corner. New guards were on duty, not Dubh and Luthais. Looking at them, she switched to Gaelic.

"Aye, I dae remember the rest o whit did pass between us this past evening."

He felt safe from Brian the Druid now, in sight of the guards, and he slowed the two of them down to a walk while they could still speak in hushed voices without being heard. And just to make sure there'd be no misunderstanding, he switched back to English.

He knew that when the guards saw the two of them

holding hands in the corridor and pausing to speak privately, word would spread throughout Laird Malcomb's Castle. It damn well better spread, because Seumas needed to know. He needed to keep his designs off her.

He brought them to a stop and turned her to face him and looked deep into her soft brown eyes.

"Something really does pass between us, Kel. It does to me. Do you feel it too, still?"

Her eyes never left his, and she nodded.

"I never stopped feeling it, Tavish."

"Oh Kelsey, I never did either. And I want to crush you to my chest right now. I want to hold you so bad."

She smiled at him then, a 'tell me about it' smile, and squeezed his hand again.

"I know. Me too. So much…"

She started drifting into him, and he almost let her. He almost said to heck with it—but he caught himself just in time and was glad, because that scenario didn't play out very well for her, here in the old time.

He held her hand between them, stopping her, and then gave her an apologetic smile, doing his best to promise things in the future with his eyes.

"Yeah, listen. While we have this chance to talk, we need to make a plan for finding the artifact and getting back home."

Slowly, she started nodding, and the pressure was off their hands from her falling into him. She righted herself, asking him a question with her eyes.

"Okay."

Oh yeah, it was definitely on once they got back. He promised that with his eyes.

"I don't think Brian the Druid will bother us if we have

Seumas and Alfred along. And Alfred's more likely to come along if you bring Eileen. So we'll try to arrange more outings like the one we had last night. Let's be on the lookout for opportunities to suggest them, okay?"

She looked down at the rock floor for just a moment, as if she were searching down there for the answer to his question. She was probably just flustered because of the dream. He knew he was. But then she answered him.

"Yeah, okay. Hey, do you think we're still going to Ireland today? Or will Malcomb cancel the trip because of the raid last night?"

He took her hand again and started them walking up toward the exit and the guards. And then he made a last comment in English before he switched back to Gaelic for their audience.

"Good thinking, that's something we can be talking about when we come out in front of the guards. Aye, we wull be gang tae Ireland, despite the raid. Laird Malcomb doesna allow the MacDonalds tae spoil our plans."

Còig deug

As she walked hand-in-hand with Tavish down the gray rock-and-grass road to Port Patrick and Donnell's ship over to Ireland, Kelsey's mind was full of the possibility of confronting Brian the Druid in his dream tonight. She had been in Tavish's dream twice. What if she thought of Brian instead tonight? Would that work? The idea reminded her of some of the Celtic legends she'd read for class.

Tavish squeezed her hand, sending a jolt of elation straight into her heart and out to the rest of her. She squeezed his hand back.

What should she say to Brian, about keeping Tavish captive?

How much anger should she show?

On the one hand, she couldn't appear weak, or once

she met the druid again outside of the dream world, he would walk all over her. On the other hand, the only strength she had was her training and her convictions— and Tavish's sword arm. She knew that if she bluffed, Brian would call her on it.

She pointed to a vendor cart loaded with warm sausages.

"Och Tavish, will ye get us a few o those?"

She saw another cart loaded with apples.

"Ooh, and some o those as well?"

Seumas got himself some breakfast too, and the three of them were quiet for a while, munching on their food.

They reached the crest of a hill, and she looked down into a rocky port full of blue water and a couple dozen ships. Hundreds of men in kilts of all colors moved to and fro, loading and unloading carpets from Arabia, tea and herbs from China, cotton from India, and for all she knew, gems from Africa. Wagons and carts and their teams of horses passed her on the road, as well.

"Which ship is Donnell's?" she asked.

Tavish pointed, but he froze in place for a moment without saying anything.

Seumas pointed then, saying, "'Tis the one wi th green sail."

She gasped.

"Can we sail wi all thon stuff pylit on the deck? Will we na sink?"

Seumas laughed.

"Nay, 'tis not even an overly large load, lass. Come, let us hurry. Donnell has that look aboot him."

Tavish hung back a bit when Seumas started walking down the Hill. Aw, he wanted a moment alone. Giving him a joyful smile, Kelsey hung back with him. But he didn't look happy, and he almost painfully moved around to the other side of her and took her other hand. What was wrong? She gave him a quizzical look.

His look was stoic as he held up his other hand, calmly whispering, "Brian the Druid must have my ring."

Seumas looked back at them.

"Will ye quit nattering on and come doon here before we raise the captain's ire?"

Tavish raised his chin at Seumas in acknowledgment and started the two of them walking again, briskly.

"Aye, Seumas, we come."

Kelsey tried to control her breathing, but she was hyperventilating. They couldn't get home without Tavish's ring. Could she get Brian to give it back to them? What would he want in exchange?

She stopped walking, resisting the tug of his hand, but not letting go.

"Let's not go on this trip, Tavish," she whispered. "Let's go talk to Brian and see if we can get your ring back."

He squeezed her hand gently, but then started walking again, bringing her along in a way that brooked no resistance.

"We canna gae against Laird Malcomb's command, Kelsey, and thare is na time tae beg aff this errand before Captain Donnell wishes tae leave. Nay, we must gae."

Walking as fast as she could to keep up with him—and huffing a little because of it, darn her habit of skipping the gym—Kelsey tried to reason with Tavish under her breath in English.

"But Tavish, we aren't going to stay here, so we don't

need to worry about following Malcomb's commands. We just need to get the ring back and find that artifact—"

He switched to sotto voice English too as he marched her along.

"If we go against his orders and then we can't find the ring or the artifact, then we're screwed, Kelsey. He can lock us up for the rest of our lives or even put us to death if he wants to. There is no guarantee of 'due process of law' in the old time." His voice softened, and she saw a tortured look on his face. "I'm so sorry I got you into this. It's my fault. I should have never brought you here. But please—you have to follow my lead so I can keep you safe. Promise me you will."

She sighed and quit resisting him, instead putting all her efforts into the long strides she needed to take to keep up with him.

"Yeah, okay, I will."

Donnell greeted them and gave them seats together, and then the crew got the ship underway. They left the relatively calm blue waters of the rocky cove and went out into the green sea.

Seumas offered Tavish his forearm, and Tavish clasped it. The two of them sat there for a moment. Seumas looked from Tavish over at Kelsey and back again.

"I'll be watching ye, MacGregor, and if ye don't tak care o her, I will."

Tavish nodded, and they let go of each other's forearms and sat amicably near each other the rest of the way, chit chatting about the other guards in the lists and their families, the stool ball game last week, how many grouse Malcomb had let them take home after the last hunting trip, and finally speculating about what they might see for sale once they reached the Irish port.

It wasn't a large ship. There was no below deck, nowhere to get any privacy. So Kelsey didn't say much, just half listened to Tavish and Seumas and watched the men sail the ship, which was entertainment enough for the short voyage to Ireland.

In about two hours, they docked at Port Beannchar.

Capt. Donnell went out on the dock and loudly proclaimed to the goods that he had aboard his ship. Every so often someone would stop and talk with him about prices and quantities, until he had his first customer—a wealthy looking man. The captain brought the customer aboard and showed him the vellum they had to sell.

Meanwhile, one of the crewmen had unpacked a writing desk for Kelsey to use. She sat poised with her quill in hand and the ship's ledger open, reading the prior sums that had been done so that she would know where to put things. It was a pretty straightforward leisure, so she felt ready.

But the captain's wealthy customer didn't agree. His Irish Gaelic was more singsong than that of the Scots, but they understood each other fine—and so did she.

The customer came right over to Kelsey and made a mocking face at her.

"Och, playing at the sums, is the lass."

Tavish got up from his seat next to her, but Captain Donnell gestured for him to sit back down. Tavish obeyed the order, but Kelsey could feel that he was ready to jump back up again at any moment.

When he spoke, the captain addressed his customer.

"Let us hae a wager. Ye can check her sums after we

finish here. Gin she makes any mistake, then yer purchase is on the house."

Talk about pressure. Kelsey swallowed and looked over at Tavish, who held up both of his hands palms down and move them apart slowly and smoothly. She nodded. He was right. She would be fine if she just took her time and was meticulous.

The customer threw back his head and laughed.

"A fine manner o salesmanship ye hae found. Ha! gin she be as guid at sums as ye think, then I will have bought more than I would hae otherwise. Fine an dandy, let us begin."

The two of them walked around on the ship, discussing this pile of vellum and that pile of cow leather and how much Donnell wanted for each piece and what discount he would give for bulk and how many hides constituted bulk…

After what was probably five minutes but seemed like an hour, the customer stepped over to Kelsey and caught her eye, seeing if she was ready to take down his order. When she nodded, he began.

"I shall tak four dozen o these hides at 18 per but wi the bulk discount for four dozen. An I shall tak three dozen o these other hides at 19 per. Pack up for me 50 sheets o vellum—did ye say the vellum was 35 per? or 45 per?"

Once she had added that up and checked it three times and made Tavish surreptitiously check it three times at the same time, she at last showed it to the captain and his customer. They each took her quill and did the same sums three times before Donnell gave her a big smile and a nod.

"Verra good, my dear." He turned to his customer.

But before Donnell could say anything, the customer was rattling off more things he would buy.

Kelsey added them all up and checked them three times and had Tavish check them three times.

The customer did his own calculations three times…

And this went on and on and on until the customer had bought everything on the ship. The crew carried it over to his ship and loaded it up for him, and then pretty much the same procedure was followed for all the merchants Donnell bought from. They had the ship emptied out and then filled up again in no time—and a large crowd of people cheered at the entertainment they had been given that day at the docks.

Before it was even time to eat the midday meal, they were finished—and Donnell's purse was fatter than it had ever been, judging by how it bulged and how big he smiled. He blew a kiss to Kelsey and then made an announcement to everyone.

"Seumas and Tavish and Kelsey and I are going up to the toon, and we will send a meal for ye, crew."

All the crewmen cheered.

Sia deug

Tavish did his best to enjoy the lively Irish musicians in the corner, as well as the meal Donnell generously bought them at a tavern, but he was impatient to be back at the castle, getting his ring back. He knew Seumas and Alfred would go with him, and a few more of the guards. Brian wouldn't stand a chance against half a dozen warriors. The druid's underhanded methods had caught Tavish by surprise. That wouldn't happen again.

Kelsey squeezed his hand under the table and put down her soup spoon.

"Dae ye no agree tavish, thon the underground is the most interestin part o Laird Malcomb's castle?"

Everyone's eyes were on him. He wiped the mutton grease off his mouth and made a face, looking to Seumas for support.

"Aw, the dungeons and docks are naught but a duty station where we dae an uncanny amount of fighting, eh Seumas?"

The large redheaded man clasped hands arm-wrestle style with Tavish on top of the table and gave him a smile so big it showed the wrinkles under his eyes.

"That be true enough of this night just past." But then Seumas dropped Tavish's hand and turned to Kelsey. "Aye, lass. And 'tis a truth that all my life I hae heard o vast treasures lurking there in the underground beneath Laird Malcomb's Castle."

Kelsey dropped her soup spoon in the soup and sat up straight.

"I knew it. I can tell by the way the halls are sae decorated, with all those etchings."

Captain Donnell's face lit up with excitement, and he gestured with his piece of mutton.

"Aye, 'tis true, 'tis true. When I was but a lad, I did hae plans tae gae doon there and plunder all the treasure, ye ken." He took a big bite and chewed it dramatically.

Everyone at the table laughed. But it was more the laugh of people who had also considered finding the treasure and keeping it for their own.

Tavish turned his head to Kelsey and gave her a look that he hoped she understood meant "What the heck are you doing? We don't want all these people thinking about going down into the underground. And we don't want Donnell asking to go with us. The fact that you can get into the secret doors is a secret, remember?"

She caressed his hand under the table. What did that mean? She smiled at Donnell.

"Seumas and Tavish and Alfred were kindly giving Eileen and I a tour o the underground last night when the MacDonalds sae rudely interrupted—"

Donnell dropped his piece of mutton on a plate and gazed at her with wide eyes.

"I hear tell 'twas ye who found Tavish in the underground castle last night, lass."

Great. Not only had she brought attention to the fact that she could find her way around in the underground, but now he would have to live down having been saved by a woman. Tavish looked around for something he could bring up to change the subject.

But before he could find a distraction, she went on.

"'Twas the strangest thing, Donnell. I was woken from ma sleep wi the sure conviction that gin I would only get up, I could walk tae where Tavish lay sleeping, havin been knockit i the head an laid oot."

This was even worse, of course. It sounded like the beginnings of all the Irish tales he'd ever heard. The musicians were on a break, and people from the other tables were starting to bend an ear toward theirs. He considered squeezing her hand to tell her to quit it, but the damage was done. He would just have to grab her and run out of the room if she got too close to revealing where she really came from. Her greed for the underground treasure hadn't made her that reckless, had it?

She tipped her tankard of ale back and swallowed half a dozen times.

"When I got ootside, I saw thon the clouds haed partit in the night, allowing the moon tae shine doon upon the courtyard. I took this rarity as a sign thon ma path was sure and I should continue."

Tavish and everyone else at the table drank down their ale now, and Donnell calmly put some coin on the table and beckoned over the server.

Kelsey picked up her bowl and drank down the rest of her soup, then wiped her mouth with the huge sleeve of her old time leine blouse.

"The guards wordlessly let me pass, and as I startit doon the corridor alone with juist ma torch for company, I had a vision o where I would find Tavish. I saw the room clearly, as gin I were already thare. Sure enough, thon was where I woke him. I'm tellin ye, I was meant tae gae an get him."

With this last line, she turned to Tavish and kissed him soundly on the mouth in a way that was considered indecent during the old time. At first he resisted, but when everyone started to cheer and whistle and carry-on, he figured what the heck, and went for it.

Truth to tell, this was the first time he'd been in a bar in the old time, and not in the castle or in a battle camp or in someone's home. Maybe the rules were different in taverns. Just in case they weren't, he put his arm around her and held her close so that no one else could grab her.

The server filled up their tankards of ale, and Seumas raised his in toast toward Kelsey.

"Och, that only I could hae my own guardian angel, tae always see me home."

"Aye!"

"Aye!"

Everyone at their table and even some people from other tables joined in the clanking of tankards, and there was much more drinking and general revelry until the four of them tottered back down the hill to the ship and got aboard.

The three crewmen had been sent on ahead with the crew's meal, and they were all done eating and had sat down to play howls, a dicing game. They all stood when their captain approached.

"Thank you for the meal, Captain Donnell."

"Aye, 'twas right good of ye."

The crewman were all smiles at first, but they began to look envious when he revealed his state of drunkenness by dramatically getting up on some crates in the stern and then gesturing for quiet so he could make an announcement.

"We sail for home, lads! Take her away."

After he said that, Donnell sat down on a bench and promptly fell asleep, snoring loudly.

Tavish looked over at Seumas, who shrugged, and then sat down beside Kelsey to warily watch the crew take the ship out to sea again. Seumas sat down on the other side of Kelsey, and for once, Tavish was glad to have him near her. With their captain unconscious, who knew what ideas the crew would get? He didn't know them half as well as he did all his fellow castle guardsmen.

Kelsey took his hand, and he made his arm as firm a hold for her as he could, then turned to smile at her reassuringly.

Come to think of it, something seemed off.

He grabbed the sleeve of the next crewman who wandered by on his way to grab one of the ropes the next time they tacked.

"Why are you sailing to the north? Port Patrick is to the

east."

A bit smaller than Tavish, the crewman stopped short of a physical reaction, but Tavish could tell he was affronted. The man just waited for Tavish to let go of his sleeve, and then gestured up at the sails.

"You can see up there that she's blowing hard to the south, aye?"

Tavish looked up. The sails were indeed billowing toward the Isle of Man.

"Aye, but what does that have to do with it?"

The crewman gave him a look as if to say, "Isn't it obvious?"

Tavish stood up straight to his full height and looked down on the man.

The crewman looked to the side for a moment and then back at Tavish.

"Because she's blowing sae hard to the south, we're taking her to the north so as not to blow right on by Port Patrick before we get that far east."

Tavish looked around at the other crewmen to see if they showed any signs that they were taking the castle guards for a ride. But none of them were snickering or avoiding his gaze. One even nodded at him in passing.

Kelsey held up her arm toward Tavish in an invitation for him to sit down again.

"It makes sense to me," she said reassuringly.

He looked all around one more time and then nodded to her and sat, taking her hand in his to lend her what comfort he could. He would be fine if he was stuck here, but this had to be frightening for her.

About a mile of rocky cliff went by on their left, pounded by the foamy waves, and then the cliffs stood still while the crew were adjusting the sails to turn the ship to the right so that they could head east.

The crewman who had climbed the mast made a guttural noise and then fell to his death atop several of the many crates on deck. An arrow stuck out of his back.

Tavish grabbed Kelsey and put her on the floor, where the side of the ship would shield her from any more arrows, and then he ran to the ship's armory, grabbed a bow and a quiver, and sought out their attackers.

Good, it was just one ship, coming toward them at a fast clip with the wind in its sails while they were stalled. He only got one shot off before the other ship was beside theirs and boarding ramps came over. But he hit his mark, and the man tumbled into the sea.

Tavish drew his sword and ran over the closest ramp, swinging at every bit of flesh that got in his way, peripherally aware that Seumas was doing the same at the other ramp, and the two crews were exchanging arrow fire.

He ducked first one sword that came at him, then another, and lunged to strike yet a third man down before he reached the other side of the MacDonald ship.

Twice he crossed over the deck, and twice he dodged better than they.

Soon, they all were buried at sea.

Seumas came over and clasped forearms with Tavish.

"Ha! Those MacDonalds didn't count on finding a MacGregor aboard our ship!"

The two of them were grinning at each other when one of their crewmen shouted.

"The lass! The lass fell overboard!"

Tavish ran back over the boarding ramp to Donnell's ship and grabbed the shoulders of the crewman who had shouted.

"Where? Where did she go overboard?"

The crewman pointed, and Tavish ran over there, grabbed the side of the ship, and looked over and down into the water. But he didn't see her.

Tavish had climbed up on the side of the ship was just about to dive as deep as he could when Seumas grabbed his arm.

"Wait. The crew say we've drifted since she went over." He pointed. "They say she's back over there toward that large jagged rock that looks like a falcon, sticking up above the rest of them along the shoreline."

Finding the falcon rock and looking for any sign of her, Tavish raised his voice, calling out to any of the crewmen who would listen.

"Can we quickly take this ship over there? Or would it be faster if I swam?"

But Seumas answered for them.

"It's too dangerous to take the ship over there—both for us and for Kelsey. She may be trying to swim to us. Look, they're anchoring here until we get back. Let's go." Seumas paused to drop his kilt on the deck before he jumped in with a splash and swam toward the rocks in a style that resembled a breaststroke more than anything else.

Tavish did the same, looking every which way as he desperately clawed the water. He had to find her. She had to be alive. He couldn't live with himself otherwise. If she...

He forced himself to concentrate just on swimming and on scanning the sparkling water and the jagged black rocky coastline for any sign of her. To convert his desperate sense of loss and despair into anger at the MacDonalds and thus into strength, so that he could swim faster. That was a warrior trick, turning sorrow into strength.

The jagged rocks were sharp, which made climbing difficult. Trying not to think of what they would do to someone unconscious, born here by the waves and dashed against them, he scrambled up onto the rocky shore and all over the jagged shoreline, calling out to her.

"Kelsey!"

"Kelsey, say something if you hear us."

Seachd deug

Kelsey clung to the rock s he'd managed to swim to. Its rough and sharp edges cut at her hands and even into her arms, right through her sleeves with every wave that washed her up against it. But she didn't yet have the energy to climb up. Swimming in a long heavy woolen dress was the most difficult physical thing she had ever done. It had been a very near thing.

A shot of joy went through her. Tavish was calling for her!

She opened her mouth to answer him, but after nearly drowning three times and swallowing and inhaling a bunch of sea water, all that came out were squeaks and croaking sounds.

"I'm here. Down here. Come get me. Please."

She felt her mind getting fuzzy. Something very like sleep but not sleep exactly was coming for her.

If only she had a flare in her pocket, like the ones her

grandparents used to make sure she had when they took her out in their motorboat. "Now I don't want to frighten you, Kelsey," her grandfather had said, "but if you should ever find yourself alone, without us around, take this flare out of your life vest pocket and pull this here and aim at the sky like this!" He'd shot the purple flare high up into the night sky like a firework, and the two of them had grinned at each other while looking at it.

If only she had some way of making a noise.

The fuzziness in her mind was growing stronger. It seemed comfortable. She struggled to remember why she couldn't just to go into it. It seemed easier. She had this gnawing feeling, this nagging feeling that there was something she should be doing to draw attention to herself. But what? She didn't even have a life jacket, let alone the whistle that usually came attached.

She started to drift, both off the rock and into oblivion.

But at the last moment before she let go of the rock, she saw a cartoon in her head that she hadn't seen since she was a child. It was a whistle fight. One character had a whistle, and the other character...

Ignoring the new cuts this gave her hands and arms, she grabbed onto the rocky shore for dear life and drew a deep breath. Puckering her lips, she prayed she could still do this, and then she whistled as loud as she could, drew another breath and whistled again. And again.

She heard two splashes behind her, and then felt strong arms lifting her off the rock into the water and then swimming with her floating on her back, the gray cloudy sky drifting back toward the craggy shore. Her body was already numb from the cold, and now her mind slowly was going numb too.

Tavish's voice intruded on her comfortable numbness.

"Kel. Stay awake. We can move you across the water, but you've got to keep your lungs full so that you stay afloat."

She dutifully took in a deep breath, held it as long as she could, and then took in another deep breath. This reminded her of swimming lessons when she was a child, with all the other happy children, glad to be allowed to spend the day at the lake...

"Breathe, Kel."

She resumed her deep breathing, trying not to drift off again into memories. But it was hard to concentrate. She was so tired, and the water felt warm now. It was hard to remember just where she was. It felt just like she was luxuriating in a warm bath...

"Breathe!"

This kept happening over and over again. She had the impulse a few times to ask how far they had to swim back to the ship, but she didn't have the energy to speak, let alone the voice.

After an interminable amount of time, Tavish was calling out to the crew aboard the ship.

"Toss us down a rope."

Before long at all, there was a splash in the water, and then Tavish was putting the rope over her and then under her arms.

"She's ready. Haul her up, lads."

Her body started to shiver when she was out of the water, and once they had her on the deck she was flopping around like a fish. Tavish was there with her soon. Holding her tight with his whole body, his legs wrapped around her, he stopped the flopping. He was shouting at the crew.

"Blankets! There have got to be some blankets on this ship!"

In a minute, it felt like someone was pulling bed covers up over the two of them. Captain Donnell's voice came through the covers muffled.

"Ye can hae the use of these Persian rugs until we can get ye up to the Laird's castle."

Tavish rolled the two of them onto one of the rugs and pulled a few more over them. His hands moved over her body then, removing her soaking wet clothes, and then the two of them were together skin to skin.

And all she felt was warmth. Blessed heavenly warmth.

He whispered to her there in the darkness while he held her tight against the cold.

"I'm so sorry Kel. So, so sorry. I should never have brought you here. I'll make it right. Somehow, I'll make it right. No matter where I have to go or how long I'll be gone, I'll make this right for you."

Kelsey tried to speak again, to tell him not to go, that all she wanted was him near her and that nothing he could go get would be better than that. But her voice wouldn't cooperate, not even to whisper. She had nothing left.

So she just clung to him, trying to make him understand that she needed him near her and that was all she needed.

His next whisper was hoarse and desperate and full of despair.

"I just hope someday you'll be able to forgive me, Kel."

She clung to him and kissed him with all she had in her the whole time the boat rocked with the pounding waves and the two of them forgot all about the crewmen stomping all over the deck as they made the ship obey them and carry them into port…

Neither of them was cold anymore.

The cries of the crewmen reached a crescendo after the ship had stopped rocking. Then they made contact with the dock, and more pairs of footsteps boarded, chatting about what to lift and where to take it.

Donnell lifted up Tavish's side of their rug bed just enough to speak into it.

"Hold on to each other and I'll have you put in the wagon!"

Panic struck her, and Kelsey looked to Tavish.

"What?"

He grabbed hold of her with all of his body again and held her tight.

"Best to believe what the captain says."

And then the crew tied two ropes around their rug bed and hoisted them up in the air. They were carried quite a ways and then dumped unceremoniously into what must have been a wagon, because as soon as the ropes were untied around their rug bed, it started to jostle around to the sound of hoof beats and general laughter.

They felt some soft things landing on top of them, which must've been their clothes. Kelsey wouldn't have believed that catcalls were the same 800 years ago unless she'd heard it for herself.

"There ye are."

"You'll probably need those where you're going."

"Unlike where ye hae been!"

Kelsey was a bit relieved when the wagon outpaced the crew's laughter, but mostly she just relaxed into the bliss of Tavish's nearness and hoped he'd forget what he'd said about going away.

The sun was setting when they got to the castle. The crew carried Tavish and Kelsey's rug bed through the service door into the kitchen and then bid them farewell amid raucous laughter.

Right there in front of the kitchen fireplace, Isabel tugged Kelsey out of the rug Tavish held around the two of them and put a thick linen night dress over her head, holding it so that Kelsey could put her arms through.

"Och, ye poor dear! I won't have any argument, ye're staying with me this night. Sorcha will see to yer wet clothes and give ye some soup to eat, and then ye really must sleep, my dear."

Tavish had already donned his dry plaid, kilting one end and blousing the other. He squeezed Kelsey's hand and kissed the top of her head.

"Aye, lass. Go on with Isabel and get ye some rest."

Kelsey tried to hold onto Tavish's hand, tried to draw him to her again so that she could whisper in his ear that she didn't want him to go anywhere, that it didn't matter if they were trapped here in the old time forever—so long as the two of them were together. But she was indeed so very tired that her grip was weak. He slipped away easily, and she still didn't have the voice to call out to him. She watched him go, hoping he would turn so that she could beckon him back to her.

But he left without looking back.

And she was not going to make a fool of herself by asking one of the women to go grab him for her. She was ashamed of herself for even thinking of that. No way was she that desperate. He would either come back, or he wouldn't.

Isabel patted Kelsey's shoulder and gave her a kind

smile when she looked at the older woman.

"Tomorrow is another day, lass. Ye are plum exhausted." She nodded to the table, where Sorcha was setting down a bowl of soup and some bread, and then sat Kelsey down there.

At first, it seemed like too much work to pick up the spoon and eat the soup, but the hot liquid felt so good on her throat. The bowl was empty in no time. So was her second bowl.

Isabel came over and helped her stand up and put a supporting arm around her waist and guided her down the hall and up the stairs to the sleeping chambers. She helped her off with her boots, and before Kelsey knew it, she was tucked into the most warm, comfortable bed ever, drifting off to sweet, sweet sleep.

But she was still aware. She let herself sleep peacefully for hours, storing up her strength, and then she dressed her dream-walking self in a white Druid robe and wished her way to wherever Brian was. Who would have thought old Celtic legends were so useful?

Oh good. He was sleeping too.

She had a moment of pause. Should she bring Tavish along? She really wanted to, wanted him with her. Longed for his company, even. But he'd walked away without looking back. There was no way she would've done the same thing, and... Best not think about that.

She nudged her way into Brian's dream the same way she'd gone into Tavish's dreams.

Brian's dream was a treat. In it, the underground Celtic castle was in its glory days. Oddly dressed people who couldn't see her wandered everywhere. Every other thing she looked at was made of gold. Oh and would you look at that.

Brian sat in the grand chamber—on the throne.

When he spotted her, he raised his chin.

"Ah, Kelsey. So nice to see you again."

She didn't bow, not even her head, just advanced right in front of him and crossed her arms.

"Perhaps you won't think so when you hear what I have to say."

He raised his eyebrows and fiddled with a golden scepter that glowed with druidic magic.

"Aye?"

Kelsey gasped.

Brian's scepter was the artifact Tavish had been sent to get. She studied it and then looked all around the room as if she were admiring the place, when really she was noting where the entrances were. She would need to go out through at least one of those in order to find out how to get in here.

Change of plans.

She was so glad she had thought and looked around before speaking. She'd been about to confront him for kidnapping Tavish and stealing his ring. Now she wished she'd come in without him being able to see her either, so she could just spy on him and find out where the ring was. Heh, she'd do that later.

She gave Brian her most solicitous smile, gesturing to the room at large.

"Aye. For I wish ye to give me a tour of your lovely underground abode."

Ha. Flattery always worked on men.

He puffed up his chest and sat up straight with his shoulders back, and gave her an indulgent smile, then put the scepter down and got up off his throne and strutted toward the elaborately marked secret door in the North corner.

"Och, I suppose I can spare the time to show you around."

Biting her cheek so she wouldn't laugh, Kelsey walked extra fast to fall into stride with him. Even though this was his dream and he was obviously enjoying showing off in front of her, she wouldn't give him the satisfaction of running to catch up. That would be just too much.

She was careful to gaze admiringly at everything they passed, in keeping with just wanting a tour. She had to bite her cheeks over and over though, because all the women gazed adoringly at Brian, and he made the winks and waves at them.

Celtic guards in bronze armor decorated with elaborate interlace nodded when they neared the door in the corner.

Darn. She didn't recognize the hallway they were in, which meant she had to endure this tour a while longer. She turned around to admire the interlace carvings on the wall, taking careful note how far down the hall they were in relation to the door, so that she could hopefully find it again.

Brian stayed puffed up, watching her admire his realm.

"You should just stay here with me, Kelsey." He stopped advancing down the hall backward, and his face changed. Instead of joy at showing off, he looked determined. Uh oh. He started walking toward her. "Aye! Stay with me." His face changed again, and this time he looked lecherous.

Kelsey didn't wait around to find out what was going to happen next in Brian's dream. She wished herself back in her own body.

But it didn't work. She was still there.

Brian had a hold of her wrist and was pulling her toward him.

She screamed.

Ochd deug

Tavish was having his favorite dream. He and Kelsey were arm in arm on their couch in the suburbs watching the antics of their two small children—a boy named Dall after his da and a girl named Linda after Kel's mom. They had just gotten back from a trip to the old time to pick up some antiques for their business, with no input and no pressure from the modern-day Druids. Tavish's twin brother Tomas and his wife lived next door and had babysat for them, and they were seated on the couch across the room...

And then his favorite dream was a nightmare, because Kelsey was screaming his name in the other room.

He jumped up off the couch, and the living room disappeared, replaced by the underground castle. At the same time, his dad jeans and sweater morphed into his kilt and his claymore. He ran.

When he got to the other room, Kelsey's screams were coming from down the connected corridor. When he got to the corridor, they were coming from a room way down at the other end. He groaned and strained, pushing his legs harder, but the faster he ran, the longer the corridor became.

No way was he going to let a dream beat him. Still running, he closed his eyes and imagined himself with Kelsey, fighting whatever was making her scream, chopping it to bits.

The corridor he was in morphed into another, finer one with lighter tan stone walls decorated from top to bottom with those designs Kelsey could read. And then she was there in the corridor—being grabbed by Brian the Druid.

Tavish didn't bother saying anything, just rushed at the man and slammed him to the floor, knocking him out instantly.

Kelsey flew into his arms and held him tight.

"Thank God you're here, Tavish. He wasn't going to take no for an answer."

A rage came over Tavish such as he'd never had before. Literally seeing red, he drew his sword in one fierce yank —

But Kelsey put her hand on his sword arm.

"This is his dream, Tavish, not yours and not mine. Haven't you heard that if you die in your dream, you die in real life? We have to be careful."

Was she for real?

"Kelsey, I don't care if he dies. He needs to die, if he would do that to you."

She shook her head no and hooked her arm around his sword arm.

"It's just a dream, Tavish. People do things in dreams all the time that they wouldn't do in real life. I do. Don't you?"

She was right. He'd already forgotten this was just a dream, even while they were talking about it being a dream. He took a deep breath and relaxed a little.

"Yeah, I suppose I do." He took a new look at his surroundings, and at her. "What are you doing here anyway, scoping out the place for more treasure? A little dangerous to come alone, don't you think?"

Whoa. She looked angry.

He backed away from her a little. Huh, well he guessed she was free to do what she wanted.

She pressed her lips together and crossed her arms, looking up at the ceiling then back at him with anger in her eyes. She glanced down at Brian, and when he didn't move turned back to Tavish and whispered.

"No, I was not scoping the place out for more treasure. I came to chew Brian out for kidnapping your sorry ass the other day, but then I saw the artifact and asked him to give me a tour so I could figure out how to get into the room where it is." She pointed down the corridor.

The artifact was in here? Tavish checked Brian himself. The man wasn't going to be moving for a few minutes, anyway. He nodded and walked where she indicated, and she followed.

When they got down to the door she'd pointed at, he ducked back and pressed his back against the wall. There were guards in the other room, and a bunch of people wandering around.

She casually walked up to the door. A little haughtily, even.

"They can't see or hear us, only Brian can."

He gestured at her with his palms up, asking how that was possible.

She mimicked his shrug and led the way into that room.

"I really don't understand how it works, just that it does. I made that a condition when I entered Brian's dream, and also when I brought you into his dream."

She brought him over to a throne, and sure enough, there was the artifact. He reached for it, but she grabbed his hand and was pulling him back toward the door.

"I don't know how long he'll stay knocked out, and we need to find your ring. In fact, we should search him for it. We also need to figure out how to get to this room, and I really think we should do that while he's still out. It surprised me when I wasn't able to leave his dream. I'm not sure if we'll be able to leave if… once he wakes up."

He kept his eyes on the scepter for as long as he could, and then finally turned to follow her. When they got back to Brian, Tavish rushed to search him, holding his other hand up to stop Kelsey from coming too close. It was there. His ring was in a pouch that Brian wore under his white Druid robes.

And then Brian grabbed Tavish's arm.

"Did ye honestly believe I could get knockit oot in ma own dream? Ha! Surprise."

Kelsey screamed again.

But Tavish asserted his superior strength against Brian the Druid and drew his arm away while at the same time making it clear that he was ready to do Brian bodily damage if he tried to stop them again.

Apparently even old time druids knew that bit about dying in your dream meant you died in real life, because Brian backed down.

It was time to get the hell out of here and wake up so they could come back with more people, overpower Brian, and get the ring and the scepter and leave. And soon, before Brian just left with those things. How much had the druid heard? Did he understand modern English? Did he know they were after the scepter? Was he aware this wasn't really just a dream? Best to assume not and hope he didn't find out.

Tavish turned to Kelsey, casually but firmly put his arm around her, and spoke as calmly as he could, under the circumstances.

"Let's go."

She nodded, but instead of dissolving Brian's dream and depositing Tavish back into his own as he had expected, she started walking down the corridor with him.

He put his mouth close to her ear and whispered.

"Get us out of this dream so we can come back in real life."

But she shook her head and whispered back to him while she scanned the walls with her eyes.

"We need to keep him in this dream as long as we can, because something tells me he'll wake up as soon as it ends."

Tavish looked back behind them, but he didn't see Brian. At least the druid wasn't following them, but not knowing where he was made Tavish uneasy.

Kelsey was still whispering.

"And anyway, we need to figure out how to get here, and this is the quickest way I can think of to do that, unless you have other ideas."

As a matter of fact, Tavish did have other ideas. Giving her a teasing look, he tested his theory by walking right up to the wall—and then through it. This network of caves have been carved out of the solid stone of the mountain, though, and so the wall he went through was very thick indeed. After about 20 feet he came into another room that he recognized, the laundry room. He looked up, which was stupid. It wasn't like he could see through the ceiling to what was above.

But he was imagining about where that other corridor that led to the scepter must be in relation to what was above this laundry room when Kelsey popped through the wall. She was in a huffy mood.

"The least you could do was tell me you were about to go walking through the wall. What if I'd been looking away? I would be back there still with no idea at all where you were."

There was no use in telling her that he'd looked to see if she was watching him. She was in that bossy lecture-y mode. Best just to keep on the task at hand.

"This system of caves over here doesn't appear to be connected to the one we were just in. It stands to reason there's another entrance to the caves where the scepter is."

At least she caught a clue and returned to the task at

hand herself. At first, she looked at the ceiling too, which made him feel better. But then she looked over toward where they'd come from, and he guessed she was doing the same as he had, imagining walking over up top from the entrance they had first used over in the direction of the scepter chamber.

She looked at him and shrugged, then turned around and *vooped* into the wall like a ghost in a horror movie. Before he could get too concerned, she *vooped* right on out, grabbed his hand, and turned around and took him with her this time.

Together, they *vooped* all over the collection of caves— finding quite a bit of treasure. It was fun for a minute, and he was laughing as much as she was. But she was getting carried away. He found out he could stop her from dragging him anymore by quite literally putting his foot down and refusing to budge.

"All right, enough of that."

She tugged at his hand.

"But we could map out the whole area in our heads —"

He refused to budge.

"We know how to get to Brian and the scepter and the ring. That's all I came for."

She clicked her tongue on the roof of her mouth, crossed her arms, and looked to the side.

"But it would only take a minute, and think how much easier it would be to do it this way than to have to dig into all those tunnels once we get home."

Was she for real?

"Don't be stupid, Kelsey! We need to get the ring back, nothing else, and Brian's liable to leave here, or to hide it,

189

or who knows what if we give him enough time. We need to make a plan that allows us to get here fast and then come back here with more people—as soon as possible."

She looked like she was going to argue some more, but then she finally nodded.

"Okay. As soon as I wish it, we'll wake up. I say we get dressed as fast as we can and rush on over to that other entrance, the one Alfred used."

He shook his head no.

"I want to bring at least Alfred and Seumas. Brian can trick one warrior into sleeping with his pixie dust, but if three of us surround him, he won't have a chance."

She got an odd look on her face and licked her lips and then nodded slowly.

"Okay. I'll stay here and keep him in the dream while you bring Alfred and Seumas and get the ring and scepter."

Was she nuts? He grabbed both of her arms and started tugging her toward the exit.

"No way. Remember why you brought me here? No way. You're coming with me. I'll not hear any argument."

She raised her chin, and his hands went through her as if she were a ghost.

"It's not like you can stop me from staying here, Tavish. I've learned some new tricks since then. I don't think I'm in danger. Go on. Bring them to that room where he sleeps."

And before Tavish could say anything else, he woke up on his cot in the castle barracks.

Naoi deug

Kelsey looked around on her own, learning quite a bit about the extensive network of caves that reached a good distance into the shore away from the cliffs. There was room to sleep a whole army down here, and it had probably been used for just that, she figured. It would take a year to catalog it all properly.

How much time did she have to mentally map out the place? It shouldn't take Tavish long to convince Seumas and Alfred to come with him. She maybe had half an hour. And as much fun as it was to go through the walls, it made more sense to go along the corridors the way she would have to back in her time.

Or would she?

She'd gone into Tavish's dream back in her time, so

that meant she could dream walk in her time. Oh. But who was there in her time who would know all these passageways? Probably only the 'they' Tavish had been talking about. She shuddered as she counted the number of turns in this particular corridor.

And there she was, on the topic she didn't want to think about.

Tavish.

For her, it had been like old times. Being with him made her feel so good. She'd given him way more than she'd planned on. He hadn't made her, either. Hadn't been demanding or expectant or anything. It had been all her. She had based her feelings on his actions instead of his words. He'd never said they were getting back together or anything. She had just assumed.

And now it was like he didn't take her seriously. Didn't want to listen to what she had to say. Now that he knew where that precious magic scepter was, she had served her purpose and he didn't need to… He didn't need her anymore.

Was that six turns now, or seven?

Groaning, she went back to the beginning of the corridor and started over. And then she *vooped* to each storage room full of artifacts and then straight up to the surface and looked for landmarks, in case the university was even more impatient than she was and wanted to dig straight down.

Finally, she'd done all of that there was to do. How much time had passed? She reached in her backpack for her phone and was about to check it for the time when she remembered it was just a dream phone, subject to the randomness of dreams. Stupid. Was there any way to tell how much real time had passed from inside a dream?

Aw, was there really any point to mapping out dream corridors? Well, she finished doing so, on the theory that corridors never changed. They were ingrained in Brian's memories, why would they change in his dream state.

Well, now she had to face it. She was dead curious to know how Tavish was progressing in his quest to get the ring back.

So she woke up. The dawn shed just enough light through her arrow slit window that she could see everything in her castle sleeping chamber clearly.

Relieved to see her clothes and her backpack (she had long since taken her jeans off and put them in her backpack, so it was just her period clothes) but a little worried that someone might have taken a look in her backpack and seen some odd things, she quickly dressed and had a look in her bag.

Satisfied that at least nothing was missing, she threw her bag over her shoulder, rushed down to the kitchen and grabbed a roll, and quickly thanked Sorcha for it as she ran out the door toward Alfred's entrance to the underground castle.

Even with gobbling her breakfast as she ran over the bone jarringly hard paving stones, she was in front of the new guards before she realized she should've thought about what to say to them. Might as well be direct.

"Hail and well met. I'm kelsey, o Tavish Macgregor's clan. Did Tavish and Seumas and Alfred gae doon thare?"

The one guard was eating an apple and he turned and spat out a seed.

The other guard gave her a puzzled look as he gestured with his thumb behind him down the dark stairs.

193

"Aye, and they are doon speaking to some feller. They said tae expect ye and tae allow ye tae gae after them, but I dinna see how ye can without a torch, lass."

Right. A torch. She thought of just going down there anyway in the dark and then grabbing her flashlight out of her bag, but she really shouldn't let anybody see that. She made an 'oh silly me' face at the guards and then ran back to the kitchen and came back with a torch, huffing a bit for breath.

"Can I light it off yer lantern?"

The guard held out his hand and she gave him the torch, which he lit for her, moving altogether too slowly.

And then the other guard took a bite of his apple and spoke to her between chews and spitting out seeds.

"Have a care on the stairs, lass. Perhaps we should call someone to escort ye."

As if she'd wait around for that. She pushed through them with her shoulder, holding the torch with one hand and her skirts with the other in order to get down the stairs without breaking her neck.

"Nay, I thank ye. Howsoever, I'll just catch up with Tavish and them."

As soon as she was out of their sight, she grabbed two handfuls of skirt at arm's length and tucked them in through the top of her belt to make the going much easier and then ran to Brian's sleeping chamber.

She heard Alfred and Seumas and Brian's and many other voices coming from the chamber when she got near, and she paused to listen.

Alfred was saying—rather nonchalantly, "...sae yer only choices are tae leave the realm or tae stay on in Laird Malcomb's service."

Someone grabbed her hand from behind, and Kelsey gasped, half turning to do one of the self-defense moves she'd halfheartedly learned and then only feeling somewhat relieved to find that it was Tavish. Why did he have to be holding her hand? It still made her melt inside, even now that she knew he'd just been using her.

He tugged on her hand, pulling her toward the entrance and whispering.

"I've got the ring and the scepter." He showed her the ring on his hand and patted the scepter where it lay concealed inside his bloused plaid. "We need to leave before they realize you're down here or that I've gone."

For once in what seemed like a long time, she agreed with him, and they made their way down to the docks and then up the other way until they got to the special corridor.

Once inside its relative safety, to her horrified embarrassment she swooned in Tavish's arms.

"Sorry. I guess now that I'm safe, it all caught up with me."

His strong arms and firm body supported her while his voice said otherwise.

"Uh huh. Come on. We just need to get down to the end of this corridor, and you'll be Dr. Ferguson once more."

She narrowed her eyes at him, even as he took her hand and walked her down to the end of the corridor.

"It's not like I ever stopped being Dr. Ferguson."

He didn't even look at her, just raised his eyebrows while he put his arm around her and raised his ring hand up and took hold of the ring with his other hand.

"Yeah, I guess that's true."

Kelsey knew in her mind that his arms were just around

her now so that his ring would transport her along with him, back to their time. So it mostly just made her mad, the way her juices started flowing when they were near like this. Mostly. Even still, it took all of her concentration not to sink into his embrace while he was still close to her.

"Just get us home already."

His body stiffened, which should've helped her withdraw, but ironically it made that even more difficult. He was so... manly.

"As you wish."

She was rolling her eyes at his sappy response when the world started spinning really fast, making her need to hold onto him so that she wouldn't fall. Darn him and his stubbornness. Why couldn't he hold on to her so that she wouldn't fall? He had to be such a gentleman all the time, making her choose to cling to him.

The world stopped spinning, and then she knew she was back in her time. It smelled different, for one thing. Not as ... natural.

"Give me a minute. I'm so dizzy."

"A minute is exactly as much time as we have before they get here."

She had forgotten that 'they' were on their way and would get here soon. Sure enough, she heard the same voices she'd heard just before the two of them escaped to the past. Those familiar voices. Only this time, she saw 'them'.

There were five, all her parents' age or older. At first glance, they looked like anyone you would see outdoors: jeans and parka or hoodie, hiking boots or sneakers, backpack or shoulder bag, water bottle.

But then she looked into their faces as they came down

the secret corridor. Wise but cunning eyes. They had never seemed creepy to her before, but she had never been the subject of their study before. These were the top echelon of professors at Celtic University. She had heard them lecture. She had looked up to them.

She was still a bit dizzy, clinging to Tavish. It was making her lean away from them.

Their leader's eyes were giving her a knowing smile even as he was clearly speaking to Tavish.

"Did you get it?"

Still keeping her firmly in his left arm, Tavish fumbled in his bloused plaid for the scepter.

Relieved to take her eyes off their leader, Kelsey turned toward the scepter and got it out.

Tavish took it in his right hand and extended it toward the professor, turning so that he stood firmly between her and them.

Their leader took the scepter and immediately examined it, then gestured to the others, who brought equipment out of their backpacks and bags.

Kelsey knew what they were doing and followed along, half in fascination at just how powerful the magic scepter was—let alone that magic actually existed at all outside of Celtic Fairy Tales—and half in dread of whatever it was they planned to do with it.

After several minutes, they packed everything up and their leader put the scepter in his bag. He looked from Tavish to Kelsey and back again, including both of them in his upward nod.

"We'll be in touch."

All of the professors turned around and confidently headed out.

Kelsey moved as if to follow them, but Tavish held her.

"Let's give them a few minutes."

She pushed against his arm.

"Fine, but give me a little space."

He let go immediately and stepped away from her, still looking up the corridor where they were disappearing around the corner.

"Yes ma'am."

She took off her backpack and set it on the floor, squatting to dig through it. First she found her jeans and pulled them on under the voluminous skirt of her Scottish plaid dress so that she could take the darn thing off. She stood there holding it for a moment, unsure what to do with it, before she decided to stuff it into her backpack—after she grabbed her phone and her sweatshirt and put it on, stuffing her huge linen sleeves into the sweatshirt sleeves.

Once she was dressed as she had been when she came into the caves just an hour ago, Tavish's hand closed around the wrist of her hand that held her phone.

"Remember, you can't tell anyone any of this."

She pulled away from him.

He let her, but he was still looking up the corridor, not at her.

She powered up her phone, glad she hadn't used it much and had kept it off most of the time.

"I'm calling my client. You know, the guy who owns this whole place—including the artifact you just gave those creeps."

He started walking up the corridor, glancing back to tell her to follow him but not meeting her eyes.

"You just called him a few minutes ago, remember?

You probably don't want to pester him. You were waiting for him to call you back."

Ug, why did he have to be so sensible? She put her backpack on but kept her phone in her hand, looking down to watch it update every few seconds as she trudged a few feet behind him up on out of the underground.

"So it's okay for you to give a golden scepter probably worth millions to those creeps, but you give me hell for wanting to upload a few photographs?"

He still didn't look back at her, didn't meet her eyes, but he took a deep breath as he kept walking up the corridor, and let it out.

"There's no way you can upload the photographs you took while we were back in the old time, Kelsey. You can't be that stupid. You know what they would do to us if you did that? You'd be accused of being a quack at best, but if anyone at all thought we were serious, they would take away any privacy we ever had a chance at having, much worse than those creeps. Yeah, they make me get them stuff, but number one, I don't have a choice, and number two, at least I do get to have a life still, unlike what would happen if you posted those photographs—"

She interrupted him, almost yelling at his back.

"I'm not talking about back in the old time, Tavish. I can't believe you think I'm that stupid. I mean the ones I took before we went, in the storage room."

They went up the stairs and out through the root cellar and across the castle way in the early morning darkness of Scotland's brooding clouds. Tavish waved to a few of the other construction workers, who were just coming out of their trailers as he and Kelsey neared Mr. Blair's trailer.

They toasted him with their tea mugs and gave her

tentative smiles, which she returned.

There was a flash of lightning.

All the men glanced up at the sky casually with their eyebrows raised, sipping their morning cup of tea and visibly wondering if they were going to get a day off for rain. Poor guys. They still had no idea what a vast underground network they were going to need to buttress so that it could be catalogued safely.

Tavish turned around then to face her, but he was still looking at the guys when he spoke.

"Well you need to wait and talk to Mr. Blair first before you do anything like that."

Kelsey put her hands on her hips and squared off against Tavish.

"I know full well what I need to do, and I don't need you telling me what that is." She hit her chest with her thumb. "I'm the senior contractor here, not you, and I will be in the owner's trailer minding his and my business until he gets here."

She was just about to turn and storm up to the door of the trailer when there was a loud crack of thunder. It made her jump a little, and stumble.

Tavish caught her before she fell, but she pushed off of him—and then did everything she could not to run into the trailer or slam the door, which she nonetheless closed behind her and locked just before the rain started hammering down.

Fichead

Kelsey looked at her phone for the time. Eight on a Saturday morning. Was that too early to call Sasha? Nah.

She called, but she had to leave voicemail.

"Sorry to bug you so early. Call me when you get this, okay? Bye."

She thought about calling her mom, but she really didn't want to discuss Tavish with her. And what was she going to say when she talked to Sasha, anyway? They had just spoken last night, and so far as her friend knew, nothing much was going on.

But everything had gone on. She'd made a fool of herself with Tavish, showing him just how much she really cared. And he had rejected her. Called her stupid. He didn't appreciate all that she'd been through at Celtic

University, all her hard study and her hard work. All that she knew now.

Well, he did appreciate it, but he had just used all her knowledge to get that magic scepter for those creepy modern druids he'd given it to. Well, good. They had what they wanted from him here, so he was free to leave. She would talk to Mr. Blair about getting a different foreman. That older man Gus should probably be the foreman anyway.

She plugged her phone in and brought up the pictures she'd taken on the sly, eight hundred years ago, putting her fingers in the venetian blinds to check the current layout of the area against them—hoping she didn't see Tavish out there.

Wow, she was really glad she had the pictures. The layout had changed a lot, and all of her mental notes from the underground exploration in her dream were based on the layout in the pictures. She got her laptop out of her bag and made herself busy on the University's inter-web, mapping her dream exploration of the Alba Palace compared to the photographs and the way the land looked now out her window.

It was an engrossing job, and it should have kept her mind off painful subjects, but every picture she looked at brought up memories of Tavish and questions about Tavish and worries about Tavish. How long had he been going to Laird Malcomb's Castle? Would he be going back there? What if something awful happened to him in that time?

Her phone buzzed and she grabbed it, relieved that Sasha would be able to keep her company.

But it was Mr. Blair.

She took a deep breath to calm her nerves and hoped it made her voice sound stable and authoritative.

"Hello?"

"Hello, Dr. Ferguson. I got yer stupendous news, and I must say I'm quite surprised and o course delighted. Can ye shew me?"

"I'm emailing you right now with the photos of the storage room we found."

"Good, good. I want tae see the storage room for myself before I decide which, if any, phootographs ye can post tae Celtic University's password protected site, ye ken?"

"Of course, Mr. Blair."

"Naught can be done i this storm, though. I'll be oot there as soon as it lets up, an we can explore yer findings."

"That sounds good, Mr. Blair. The palace is quite a bit more extensive than you thought, and I'm looking forward to showing you. To give you an idea just how much more extensive, I'm drawing up blueprints, because there's no way I could simply explain it to you."

"I've just received the phootographs, and I dinna quite see what ye mean. Sure, there are many artifacts in this room, but the room itself is rather small, is na it?"

Kelsey sighed. Tavish would know exactly what to say to Mr. Blair. It was apparent he had been here dealing with him for a long time.

But she didn't need Tavish. She had been taught how to deal with clients—although admittedly not how to explain to them how she knew something she couldn't have known unless she had traveled back in time...

She thought carefully about what she could tell him.

"When you get here, I can show you the many secret

doors in that one passageway you've found. I've opened a few, and the language of the carvings tells me there are many, many more. Your construction crew will come in very useful making sure everything is structurally sound down there so that exploring can be safe…" An idea hit her, and she ran with it. "This project has grown in scope so much that I wish to bring in a colleague, Dr. Sasha Swain."

"A colleague from Celtic University?"

"Yes, we were there together and both got our doctorates at the same time. She lives here in Scotland, so it wouldn't take her long to get out here to the site, and I'm going to need her help. I just hope she's available."

Mr. Blair sounded excited on the phone, and she tried to focus on all the things that made this project exciting—except for Tavish.

"I'll have tae see the secret doors ye're talking about, o course, and this room full of artifacts whose phootographs ye've sent me, but if that all works oot as ye say, then I see nae problem with bringing in yer colleague—and perhaps a few more colleagues, just sae this dig does na take ten years tae finish."

Now her training kicked in, and she was on more or less familiar ground, getting more confident with each sentence.

"We can make a spectacle out of the project itself, Mr. Blair. That can bring in some money for you off the tourist trade. Maybe you should build an inn nearby…"

A few minutes later, she hung up the phone, pleased with herself and really hoping Sasha would be able to come help.

Ooh, and there was a text from her friend:

"Almost there, talk then!"

She texted Sasha back:

"In the big gray trailer out front."

Kelsey drew up one of the blinds and gawked at the pouring rain. Was Sasha even crazier than she remembered? Oh well, worrying wasn't going to help. And having her friend here was just the thing she needed to get over her disappointment about… no, to get excited about this project. It was going to be so fun! This was both of their dream project, supervising a huge dig in Scotland.

But as she continued to create the blueprints, she wondered what Alfred and Seumas were saying to Brian the Druid and how Eileen would react when she heard Kelsey had fallen into the sea and been rescued by Tavish and Seumas…

Yeah, Tavish probably would be going back to the old time, and he was good at improvisation and could explain her absence in some way. Maybe say she was moping somewhere. She could envision his face as she told Seumas that, could envision Alfred rolling his eyes at the idea and then turning to appreciate Eileen for the sweetheart she was. And then Tavish would get them all excited about some other quest they needed to go on—so that he could verify the outside location of a room they needed to dig into here in the present…

But no, he wouldn't be around to help her in that way if he chose to leave because he couldn't take her being in charge. She sighed, and her hands stopped moving on the keyboard. Her eyes drifted to her Celtic University ring. Yeah, she had book learning, and it was paying off in great ways, being able open the secret doors—and that Celtic Fairy Tale trick of sneaking into people's dreams.

But it would be so much more fun with Tavish around.

For reasons that made sense, not just sentimentally.

Tavish knew the old time just as well as the present day. He walked right in with confidence and that sexy swagger where she would always seem out of place. He had lived there. He understood history in a way that no one else she knew did. Yeah, there were sensible reasons to want Tavish around.

She didn't only want him around because he knew her better than anyone else, even Sasha. And not just because he always protected her and watched out for her, and kissed her like he meant it…

Even with all her rationalization, she concentrated hard enough to get the blueprints almost done in a few hours, but she should have been much faster at this. Too much of the time, instead of working at the computer, she played with her university ring, the symbol of her lofty educational distinction, slipping it on and off and turning it around and around.

There was a loud knock on the door.

Kelsey jumped, and then she lifted up the blinds.

Sasha smiled and waved at her through the rain, holding up a plastic bag from the Chinese restaurant in town.

Kelsey jumped up and let her friend in, giving her a big hug and taking the plastic bag from her and rushing with it to the microwave.

The food smelled wonderful. Kung Pao, if she wasn't mistaken.

Yep. And rice to go with it.

She broke the metal handles off the cartons and stuck the whole things in the microwave to heat it all up, then hurriedly dished it into two bowls and grabbed two beers out of the fridge.

"Make yourself at home. This is the client's trailer, and *he* will be here once the rain lets up. I can't believe you drove out here in that downpour, but I'm glad you did."

Sasha had sat down on the couch, and Kelsey plopped a bowl and a beer on the coffee table in front of her, keeping the other ones as she sat down next to her friend.

"Sasha, I want you to be my partner on this project. Can you spare a couple years?"

Aon air fhichead

Tuffy ran up to Tavish as soon as he entered his trailer, and he scooped up the little dog and petted him, then brought him back over to Gus, who was the oldest member of the construction crew in addition to being his roommate.

"He earned his name today, Tuffy did. Stood up to a mastiff over castle way."

Gus held out his arms, and Tavish placed the little dog in them, where he was tenderly held. Gus then rocked him much like one would a baby—which was always comical, Gus was so huge.

"Aye, the woman said so much when she brought him

back to me." Gus nuzzled his face into Tuffy's head and spoke to the dog. "Yes she did. Yes she did."

"Sorry you had to speak to her."

The old Scot looked up at him with his bushy gray eyebrows wrinkled.

"Why do ye say that?"

Tavish wrinkled his own brow in return and reached over to pet Tuffy.

"You don't find her even a bit high and mighty?"

Gus pursed his lips and raised his eyebrows.

"Nay, far from it. She was right nice aboot bringing Tuffy back to me. She didn't have to do that." And then he spoke to the dog again, still jiggling it in his arms like a child. "Don't you be running off again now. I was so worried." Eyes back on Tavish, he said, "What makes you say she's high and mighty?"

Tavish went into their tiny little kitchenette to heat up some leftover fish and get himself a cup of tea. He held up an empty cup toward Gus, who shook his head no.

"Well you know we used to know each other when we were younger."

"Aye, it's plain to see in the way you are with each other, even if you hadn't told me."

"Yeah, well most of the time she treats me the same as always, but every once in a while now, she acts like she knows better than me—"

Gus laughed. "Bothers you, does it?"

"Well, yeah."

Gus shook his head. "Son, she *does* know better than you—"

Tavish almost dropped his teacup. Was the man serious? "She doesn't know the first thing about construction work."

"Nay, but she doesna need to. She has you for that, and us."

"Well what does she know so much about then?" Even as he said this, Tavish knew he was being stupid. She knew all kinds of useful druidic things. But did Gus know that? And why was Gus taking her side, anyway?

Gus sighed and calmed poor Tuffy, who'd been a bit startled by Tavish's tone of voice.

"Bit rough to see when it's a woman—and a fine one at that—however, she *is* a suit, Tavish. She has a doctoral degree. She'll be second in charge of this job after the owner, and I wouldna be surprised if she brought on people who'll be third and fourth. When you've been around as long as I have, you'll be able to see these things coming. But I thought I'd better warn you. She does know better, and it'll be her job to tell you so."

Whatever. But wow, Gus really did know something. Were the druids on him, too?

"What makes you think there's a big enough job here to require a second in command, let alone a third and fourth? You do know that stuff we found in the basement was just trinkets made in the 70s by some hippies, right?"

"Aye, that it was. But you aren't from around here, Tavish. You didn't grow up with the stories about how the ancient home o the kings of Alba resides beneath these cliffs here. You see, Mr. Blair must think there's some truth to that, or he wouldna have tried so hard and fought so long to get this land back after his drunken ancestor let it fall out of the family hundreds of years ago. This will be a big find. Depend upon it. Won't be long before news crews are out here covering it. But getting back to your friend—uh, Kelsey?"

"Yeah, her name's Kelsey, but now she seems to prefer Dr. Ferguson."

Gus nodded sideways.

"I suppose if I spent seven extra years in school to get a doctorate, I'd prefer to be called Dr. as well." He raised his eyebrows at Tavish.

"I guess." Yeah, Gus did have a point.

"I'm just saying maybe it's you who are na being a verra good friend, here."

There was a loud bang on the door, and the voices of Brody, Lyle, and Gavin could be heard outside, along with a general hubbub that said there were more guys with them.

"Are you in there, Tavish?"

"We're on to have a party because of this rain."

"Aye, and because of the boss being away."

Gus smiled at him, and Tavish went over and let the guys in. It was crowded with 10 of them in the small trailer, but they had brought whisky, so he supposed he could stand it. There were far from enough chairs, even with the small sofa, but the men who didn't get seats made do with sitting on the sofa arms or leaning on the kitchenette counters.

As they passed the bottles around, Tavish thought about what Gus had said.

Dhà air fhichead

An hour before sunset, it had still been raining, and so Mr. Blair had said he would come the next day and was eager to meet Sasha. Sure enough, the next day dawned dreary but dry, so their high-tech equipment from the university would be able to survey the land and mark out the underground castle's likely entry points. Which would all be recorded and stored away in the university's records, of course.

Kelsey and Sasha had microwaved frozen breakfast sandwiches and donned their suits—Sasha kept one in her trunk for just such emergencies—and they were getting their equipment ready to go out and start surveying while they waited for Mr. Blair to arrive.

Kelsey felt much better after a good night's sleep.

"Now don't let Tavish give you any grief," she told

Sasha. "I'm not going to. He probably won't, though. He and I are having a little fight, but really he's a nice guy. I'd be surprised if he said anything mean to you at all. No, that's going to be all for me, lucky me. But yeah, if he does, just realize it's because he's mad at me. It won't be about you—"

Sasha elbowed her in the side gently.

"Quit it. I'm sure it will be just fine. You're over the fight, and he probably is too. In fact," she picked up Kelsey's purse and walked her over to the bathroom and handed it to her, "I think you should do your makeup. You never know."

Kelsey rolled her eyes at her friend, but doing her makeup did sound like a good idea. After all, she wanted to look put together when she presented her blueprints to Mr. Blair, and likely he would have her explain the project to the crew.

Half an hour later, they were immersed in their task of showing all the land to the equipment when Kelsey recognized Mr. Blair's voice.

"I like that, ye got right tae it first thing in the morning." With Tavish trailing slightly behind him, the client walked up to Sasha and offered to shake hands. "Hello, I'm Keith Blair, the new owner of these premises. And you must be Dr. Swain. Dr. Ferguson here speaks very highly of you."

Kelsey couldn't help turning her eyes toward Tavish while Sasha returned Mr. Blair's pleasantries. He gave her a tentative smile, which she returned.

Mr. Blair turned his attention toward her and gestured at all their equipment.

"So what's this all aboot, then?"

Kelsey showed him the tiny monitoring screen.

"The equipment is finding the Alba castle's likely entrance points, see?"

Mr. Blair peered into the little monitor, but then Tavish put a hand on his back, taking his attention away.

Kelsey felt her hackles rise, and she spun on her heel, preparing to get some distance between herself and Tavish—and unfortunately between herself and Mr. Blair. She was going to have to do something about Tavish. She did not want to do this job under these working conditions. It was demeaning. She felt more like an errand girl than a doctor.

But then she heard Tavish's voice.

"While this equipment is grand, and we will need its readings for all the work ahead, it's much more imperative now that you let Kelsey show you the storage room we found—isn't that right, Kel?"

Sasha gave her an 'I told you so' smile before Kelsey could answer.

She gave Tavish a 'thank you' smile and then turned to Mr. Blair with an expression she fought to keep professional, but which she knew was all excited.

"Oh yes, absolutely. In fact, let's go over there right now."

She and Sasha had been sensible enough to wear their hiking boots with their suits, so all four of them went right over to the hatch door above the root cellar. Tavish got it open and gestured for her and Sasha to go down first in their skirts, which they did, but then she heard Tavish talking to someone new up top.

"Go on down and introduce yourselves to Dr. Ferguson and Dr. Swain," she heard him say.

She looked at Sasha, who shrugged.

And then the two of them watched a third woman come down the ladder next. She was stylishly dressed, but in slacks, and her hair and makeup were Hollywood grade.

Bile rose up into Kelsey's mouth. If Tavish had a girlfriend…

But the woman no sooner made it down than two more strangers came down the ladder, men this time, with big backpacks on. They started to open their backpacks while the woman looked at all the nooks and crannies in the 10 x 10 stone root cellar with interest.

The woman finally turned toward Kelsey and Sasha and held out her hand.

"Right, sae ye're the Dr. Ferguson who will show us how tae get in the secret doors, eh?"

Kelsey made a face that hopefully showed how puzzled she was, but she shook the woman's hand.

"Do I know you?"

The woman laughed and went on to shake Sasha's hand.

"Oh, ye're American, and ye dinna have a clue who I am, dae you?"

Kelsey looked at Sasha, who shrugged again, so she looked back at the woman and shook her head no.

The woman visibly admired Kelsey and Sasha's Celtic University rings and then turned to the two men, who were unpacking equipment.

"I'm Gisa Sutherland with BBC Scotland, and we're here tae dae a story on ye, Dr. Ferguson, complete with movie cameras documenting how ye open these secret doors."

Tavish and his kilt came next down the ladder, which

thankfully was on the other side of the small room. He spoke up toward the top of the ladder, where Mr. Blair's feet could be seen.

"I can't wait for you to see this, Keith. She had it open in just a few seconds."

Once everyone was down, Mr. Blair gathered them around the secret door with the camera crew's lights blaring.

"Well nae, Dr. Ferguson, I reckon ye'd better show us yer magic."

Her eyes went to Tavish's, and the two of them shared a look which savored the excitement and the awe they had felt the first time she did this.

And then she explained to Gisa and the camera crew and the rest of Scotland and probably the world how she had read the Celtic interlace symbols and known this was a secret door.

She opened it and gave everyone a tour of the underground space you could get to without opening any more secret doors—with all of its arcane runes and ancient items. She even let Sasha explain some of it, once they got to the storage room.

BBC Scotland's camera crew were as shocked as she had been, to find that cellular connections worked down here. They'd been able to do some of the segments live.

If Kelsey was any judge, Mr. Blair was glowing almost as much as she was from all the attention the project was getting, and he insisted that Kelsey show the camera crew her blueprints and explain just how large she thought Alba Palace was.

By the time the folks from BBC Scotland departed, the sun was setting in a trail of sea sparkles leading to the distant view of Ireland.

Mr. Blair turned to Kelsey and Sasha out in front of his trailer.

"I'll be gang back into toon where I've got a motel room for tonight, but tomorrow I'll get ye ladies yer own trailer brought oot here. I'll see that ye each hae yer own room. Any ither amenities in particular that ye'd like?"

Kelsey just shook her head no, all the while smiling at Tavish.

Sasha gave Kelsey a playful little shove and led Mr. Blair over to his car, which was parked on the other side of the trailer.

"Is it possible we could each have our own bathroom as well? And do any trailers come with full refrigerators? What about built-in espresso makers? And if this is going to be a new trailer, then I prefer blues to neutral colors…"

Alone with Tavish at long last after just stealing glances at him all day, Kelsey hurried over to him, talking before he could say anything.

"Thank you so much for today, Tavish."

He twinkled his eyes at her and raised his eyebrows as if to say, 'Whatever for?' Which let her know it was okay, and they weren't fighting anymore.

She moved closer to him, reaching out, and he opened up his arms so that they were soon holding each other close, watching together as the sky and the sea grew red.

She spoke with her head against his chest, hearing his heartbeat.

"Only you could have explained all that to the TV station ahead of time, and it was the sweetest thing you could have done for me today, making sure the world knew I had something to do with this discovery. Thank you so much."

He caressed her back.

"You're welcome, Kel. Sorry it took me so long to see how much you know, and how much you can do. I'm so proud of you, and I'm so sorry I didn't let you choose whether I'd leave or not, all those years ago. I was miserable without you, and I'm so sorry if I made you miserable by leaving. I thought I was doing the right thing, but now I see that all I did was make you lose faith in me."

She squeezed him tight.

"Apology accepted. Now it's my turn. I'm so sorry for the way I treated you in our time's yesterday, like some stupid construction worker who couldn't possibly know anything about ancient ruins."

He kissed the top of her head as he held her close and then laid his head down on top of hers, enveloping her.

"There was no way you could have known I'd been back to the old time, Kel. And for all you knew, I was just a jerk who disappeared from your life and hadn't spoken to you in seven years. Your behavior made perfect sense."

"True, but I'm still sorry. And you're at least as responsible for the discovery of Alba Palace as I am."

He started them rocking from side to side and raised his head up, then beamed a smile at her when she met his eyes. He lowered his mouth to her ear and whispered.

"But thanks to you, I got the old druids their scepter in two days instead of two years, and they'll be off my back awhile. You did me a much better favor than I did you."

She pulled away until he could see her face and know that she was sincere.

"Still, I'm going to find a way to give you credit for this discovery, too."

He studied her face, equally sincere.

"I don't need credit with the world, Kel, only with you."

Her face broke into her biggest smile.

"You have all the credit in the world with me."

He lifted her and swung her around, then settled comfortably with her still raised up so they were face-to-face, with his arms around her waist.

"Will you give me a lifetime with you to spend it?"

Lost in his eyes, all she could do was nod a vigorous yes before she was kissing him.

Epilogue

Seumas looked around for Tavish as he and Alfred and the other men escorted the druid Brian up to his audience with Laird Malcomb. That MacGregor had been here just a moment ago. Where could he have gotten to?

And then when they were almost up out of the caves, passing through the washroom, Tavish came up from behind out of nowhere and joined them, as he was wont to do in this area. Come to think of it, Seumas had been meaning to ask him about that. But not when others could hear them.

They had passed on up by the entrance guards and were in the castle town when the prisoner tried to make a break for it, lunging between him and Tavish.

He met eyes with MacGregor over the druid's head when they both threw their knees out to stop him, making the man double over and retch. They shared a grim satisfied smile, and then each took an arm and hoisted the prisoner kicking and screaming between them all the way to Laird Malcomb's office, where he ordered the druid locked into the tower, which they did with satisfaction.

The group of men paused outside the tower door while their leader spoke with another head guard.

What was it he was going to ask Tavish about again? Oh well. Must not have been important. Instead, when he turned toward Tavish, he asked the man the first thing that came to his mind.

"Is Kelsey well after her ... dunking?"

Ah, and there it was in the man's eyes. His love for the lass, aye, but also his certainty of her love for him. Seumas was happy for them.

Tavish nodded with a contented smile.

"Aye, that she is. Nae harm done."

The man's eyes had a faraway look to them. Guessing he was remembering a pleasant time he had spent with his woman, Seumas felt the urge to be elsewhere. Not because he envied the man and felt alone in the company of one so happy, no. Just because he had better things to do.

But Tavish started patting all around his waist with a bit of a stricken look on his face.

"My sporran. Must've fallen. Had it when I went down with you to go get Brian. Need to retrace my steps." He took off at a brisk pace down the hallway, looking down at the floor.

Seumas went about his duties with the squadron of guards, expecting Tavish to rejoin them at any moment, with his sporran once again around his waist by its cord. The more time went by without that happening, the more concerned and curious he grew.

Finally, he made an excuse and ran off after that MacGregor. After descending the stairs, he encountered the man, but he wasn't alone. Kelsey was with him, and the two of them looked very happy, and again he was happy for them, but the other woman along with them distracted him.

Wrapped up in Tavish's spare plaid as if it were a cloak, she walked with as much certainty as Kelsey did—a true rarity in a woman. How remarkable for there to be two such women in his acquaintance. She spoke Gaelic with an accent like Kelsey's, but stronger. They must have come from the same glen. She spoke with confidence as well, even though she faltered for words as if Gaelic were not her true language.

And she was a beauty. Her hair was as red as his, and her skin was clear and fair between the redheaded sun dapples. She was tall and lean and strong—he could tell even through the cloak she wore.

And she was staring at him in awe.

The End
Of Tavish's book

From the Author

Thanks so much for reading Tavish's story to the end. I'm glad you enjoyed it.

I wrote about Tavish's highland origins in the Renaissance Fair series

It's a druid fantasy story about Tavish's parents. It shows you why Tavish has to serve the Druids. His parents have quite a bit more leeway to experiment with time travel.

You can sign up to be notified when Seumas and Sasha's book, book two in the Dunskey Castle series, is available at **janestain.com**

If you want a daily dose of the highlands — photos (castles, coos, mountains, lochs, men in kilts), music, and history — then I'll see you on Facebook if you like my page:

https://www.facebook.com/RenaissanceFaireKilts/

All my best,
Jane Stain

from

The Renaissance Faire Series

published as

Kilts at the Renaissance Faire

Copyright © 2015 Jane Stain (Cherise Kelley)
All rights reserved.
ISBN-13: 978-1541078420
ISBN-10: 154107842X

Emily loved the Renaissance Faire. Where else could she see a Shakespearean play performed authentically, with men playing the female parts? Minstrels strolling about with mandolins, asking a kiss for a song?

Where else could she see men in kilts?

And with her freckled skin, she felt like she fit in here, more so than at any other hangout she'd been to. She ran from booth to booth, getting a juggling lesson here, trying to walk a tightrope there—

"Emily, look at these dresses."

Her tiny brown best friend Evangeline was in graduate school too, majoring in elementary education, while she herself was preparing to lead a high school drama department.

Emily joined Vange in a booth made of dyed burlap walls.

"They're beautiful, Vange."

A faire employee wearing one of these outfits came up to them.

"They are not dresses, milady, but bodices and chemises with two skirts to wear with them, one over the other and tucked up out of the dirt. This is the clothing of our peasant women, milady."

Emily looked around uncertainly for a fitting room.

"Could we try a few on?"

The costumed lady nodded enthusiastically

"Certies. Do come stand over here in the corner. I shall hold up this blanket, and the two of you can change behind it."

The faire person said this rather loudly, and a small crowd gathered outside the booth. In particular, Emily noticed this one muscular guy with a dog tattooed on his arm.

Still, the outfits were lovely, and Emily loved the idea of wearing one the rest of the day so that she fit in at the faire. It reminded her of her own drama student days, back in high school.

She looked at Vange.

Her friend winked.

So they turned their backs to the blanket and put the outfits on. They heard several cat calls from their audience, but they could see in a small mirror in the corner that the blanket stayed put the whole time.

The two of them admired each other in the outfits, which didn't show any leg at all, but a whole lot more cleavage than either of them was used to. The faire person had insisted that they lace their bodices up tightly.

Vange gave her a huge grin.

"OK, we'll take these."

The costumed employee looked at Emily for confirmation.

Emily stared at her new cleavage in the mirror.

"Yes, we will definitely take these." She looked at the faire employee again. "One sec while we get the money, OK?"

The woman looked surprised, but she nodded. She kept holding the blanket up too, probably because phone calls were anachronisms. While she waited, she taunted their audience with descriptions of how good her customers looked, wearing her wares.

Once Emily was done on the phone, she smiled to hear that Vange was having the same trouble she'd had. Now that her mom had finally answered her call, her friend wasn't quite whining, but almost.

"But I *do* work. Graduate school isn't a picnic, you know ... No, I *am* grateful that you pay for school ... *Please?* Mom, wait till you see it. I won't ask you for any more money all summer, OK? ... Yes, I promise." Vange handed her debit card to the faire woman.

Emily had been waiting to make sure Vange got the money too. No sense in only one of them having a costume. That wouldn't be any fun. She handed her debit card over.

"They'll work now."

After they paid, Emily and Vange stowed their T-shirts under their voluminous skirts in the waistbands of their shorts, and the blanket went down.

With smug smiles on their faces at how authentic they now looked compared to the rest of the fairgoers, the two of them turned around to face their audience.

Only, instead of sunburned tourists in shorts, Emily and Evangeline faced a whole clump of whooping Scots highlanders in kilts.

***

Emily stared at the highlanders. In addition to their thick woolen great kilts, they all wore two-handed longswords and heavy boots of cowhide. They had on homespun linen shirts similar to the chemise she now wore, but their sleeves were wide at the wrist and their shirts laced up on their chests. Most of them had long hair and beards.

They all wore big smiles.

Her eye kept drifting to one Scot in particular who stood next to their leader. He stood out, but she couldn't put her finger on how. He was gorgeous, of course, but they all were.

Their leader shouted out with a big grin.

"Do a dance for us, ladies."

Sensing herself blush, Emily felt rooted to the cloth floor of the booth. She glanced over and saw that her normally outgoing friend Vange wasn't doing any better.

And then the man her eye was drawn to spoke, and she knew why he stood out. The leader was trying, but this one had a perfect Scots accent. He must be from there.

"Aw, Ian. Let us show these fine ladies we know how to have a good time, eh lad?"

Ian raised his eyebrows and then grinned.

"Fair enough, Dall."

Emily sighed with relief.

And then she was giddy when Dall spoke again.

"Faire ladies, we pray you please accompany us at our clan dance, which does begin soon."

Another quick glance at Vange revealed that her friend very much wanted to dance with these sexy bare-legged men. Emily did, too. She grabbed Vange by the elbow and steered her into Ian, while Emily placed herself next to Dall.

The authentic Scotsman held out his forearm for Emily's hand, the way men did in old movies when they walked with women.

For some reason, this made Emily shy.

What in the world is wrong with me? It's just his arm.
It wasn't like he was groping her or anything.

And then, when Emily stepped closer and took Dall's arm to walk with him, her stomach fluttered.

The band of Scots lined up two by two and paraded through the dirt streets of the fake English village that had been constructed for the Renaissance faire, out in a fallow field.

Dall held his arm out for her the whole way. She was glad for more than one reason, as she often had to steady herself. He paused when there were holes in the road so that she took notice and watched her footing.

He made small talk, so that she didn't feel awkward walking with him.

"Do you see the giant there, lass?"

Emily followed his gaze over the heads of the people in the street until she saw the giant. It was about 15 feet tall, held up by four English peasants who walked under it and followed by a few dozen more. They were singing, but too far away for Emily to hear.

She turned back to Dall.

"Oh yeah. Why are they parading a giant puppet around?"

He wrinkled his brow as if everyone knew.

"He is the Green Man."

She gave him a questioning look.

"Oh, do you not know the Green Man, then?"

She shook her head no.

"He does bring the springtime—in the minds of the farmers, you ken."

"Oh. OK, that makes sense, I guess."

But even with his small talk, Emily's stomach fluttered the whole time, which was silly. Dall was being a perfect gentleman. He wasn't too close or trying to grope her or anything. She had heard rumors of that sort of thing happening at faire. No, although he was way more attentive to her as a woman than any stranger she had ever met, Dall was nice.

As they walked, more and more Scots joined the parade, until there were at least a hundred of them, maybe more, about equal parts men, women, and children.

Whenever someone joined them nearby, Dall introduced her.

"This is Emily," he'd say, and then he would tell her their names.

All of which she promptly forgot, she was so distracted by the faire. OK, and by this gorgeous man at her side.

But the faire was distracting, wonderfully so.

Everywhere she looked, something was going on.

Brightly costumed dancers held ribbons attached to the top of a huge pole in the ground. As they danced around it, their ribbons formed a braided pattern that coated the pole.

People dressed in black with skeletons painted on them danced around with hourglasses.

There were even knights in armor riding horses in the distance.

Her ears caught a new tune every dozen feet they walked: mandolins, wooden flutes, deep resonant drums, a bunch of sea dogs singing about Bengal Bay...

A good many of the people she saw were dressed in costumes. Some of these were authentically historical—peasants, mongers, nobles, foreigners—but many people wore fanciful costumes—wizards, elves, fairy princesses, Amazon women warriors in furs and little else...

The parade of Scots paused when they came to one of

several large outdoor theaters set up all over the faire. It had a large wooden stage that she thought could fit a whole orchestra. Straw bales had been lined up in rows for seating, and hundreds of fairgoers already sat there, eating turkey legs and drinking beer out of large paper cups printed to look like metal tankards.

But Dall didn't make any motion to help Emily sit down on one of the straw bales.

And the Scots were parading right up onto the stage. The musicians were in the front, and now they played as they marched up the steps, bagpipes and drums mostly. The bagpipes were loud.

Before Emily could get used to just how loud the bagpipes were, the whole parade was moving again. Up the stairs to the stage.

Dall was smiling and waving at the fairgoers on their straw bales, and they were waving back.

The next time he glanced her way, she spoke to him.

"Where shall I sit to watch your clan dance?"

The way he looked at her then left nothing to the imagination, though he did nothing rude. It was more … yearning. Inviting. Questioning?

"Oh no, lass. You'll no be sitting. I intend to take you as my partner."

Why can't I look him in the eye?

"Your … partner?"

And why did my voice have to squeak just then?

In that moment, she realized something that she thought answered her question from earlier, about why he stood out:

Dall was infinitely more confident in himself than the college guys she was used to. Heck, he was more confident than her professors, and that was saying something.

He gave her a warm smile.

"My partner for the dancing, lass."

"Oh."

He helped her up the steps onto the stage, and the two of them followed the procession until they were facing the audience and clapping with the rest of the clan while three young women held their skirts up out in front of them and jumped up and down to the beat of the bagpipes and drums.

In her element on stage, Emily clapped and smiled at the audience while she talked to Dall out of the side of her mouth.

"I don't know how to dance like that."

She gestured at the three women.

"I've seen River Dance a dozen times, but that doesn't mean I know how. And I'm still wearing sneakers."

But he pulled her forward into a dance set of four couples.

"Do not fret, lass. We will not be dancing in that style. It will be easy. Just follow my lead."

They all bowed to each other.

And then the music started, and along with it the dance.

It was much like the square dancing Emily had done in fourth grade—only to bagpipes instead of banjos—and once she relaxed, she enjoyed it.

No one called the moves, but Dall was right. All she had to do was pay attention and let him guide her. There was no skipping involved, thank goodness, and her underskirt was long enough that it hid her sneakers. Most of the time.

When Evangeline and Ian appeared opposite herself and Dall in their next dance set, Emily realized she had forgotten all about her friend.

She smiled at Vange in apology.

Vange gave her a knowing look in reply.

Emily rolled her eyes at that.

But whenever the two friends locked elbows for a turn, Vange whispered something different in Emily's ear:

"Go for it."

"He's delicious."

"If you don't want him, then scoot over."

The first two comments just made Emily laugh at her friend, but the third one made her seriously consider. She looked over at Dall, who was swinging by Ian's elbow.

He smiled at her the way a cat smiles when it is warm and fed and content at home in winter, in front of a roaring fireplace.

She couldn't help smiling back at him the same way.

"I thought so." Vange was laughing now.

***

When the Scottish clan's dance show was over and the audience was applauding thunderously, the highland woman nearest to Emily grabbed her hand and pulled her forward into the line of female performers, who all curtseyed. What happened next explained why she had done this. The women backed up and dropped hands to let the men through.

The kilted men all went out to the front of the stage, formed a line, put their arms around each other—and did a can-can dance to the drums.

Ba boom, kick

Ba boom, kick

Ba boom, kick

Ba boom, kick

Emily knew the can-can wasn't a 'period' dance for

this faire, but the audience loved it. Too bad she was behind the guys and couldn't see better, but because there were only amused faces in the audience, Emily figured the performers were not authentically (un)dressed under their kilts...

She looked over to see Vange's reaction.

Her friend was whistling at all the hot guys through her forefinger and her thumb.

Their eyes met, and they gave each other huge silly grins.

This was the most fun they had ever had at renfair, and this was their third summer break here together. There were ten more weekends of this faire, and Emily had a feeling she wanted to come back this year. Maybe all ten weekends.

That feeling grew more intense.

Dall was once again at her side, holding his arm out to help her go down the steps off the stage. He made no move to let go of her once they were down, either.

Ian came over with Vange on his arm, and two more couples followed. One of the women had a container that reminded Emily of a bota bag, and she used it to fill metal tankards for them all to drink from.

Emily took a huge gulp when she got hers.

"It's just water."

The woman who handed her the tankard dropped her fake Scots accent and whispered to Emily.

"Yeah, we don't really drink alcohol during the day out here at faire. It's liable to give you heat stroke, especially with all this heavy wool clothing we have to wear."

Emily could see the sense in that, but she was a little disillusioned. All the faire people seemed to be happily drunk all the time. Still, she downed her water and asked for more.

The woman refilled her tankard twice before she stopped thirsting, and then she handed Emily and Vange what looked like cloth bags.

"Here, put these muffin caps on, to keep the sun off your heads."

Looking around, Emily now noticed that all the faire people had hats on, and most of them wore muffin caps like these. The color went OK with her dress, so she put it on and helped Vange put hers on. Unlike the faire woman, though, Emily let her hair hang out from under the muffin cap, figuring she would look better that way.

Vange did the same, winking.

Putting his arm firmly around Vange's shoulders, Ian addressed Vange, Emily, and Dall, and incidentally the other two couples.

"We're going to see Short Shakespeare. Come with us."

Emily had turned to ask Dall if he wanted to go when she saw him bowing to her with his hand out for hers. It was over-the-top dramatic, but also sweet.

Feeling her face spread into a silly grin, she made a big show of swooning with her forearm on her forehead before she took his hand, thankful again that her drama training got her through her usual shyness when it came to action, if not speaking.

She put her hand in his offered one, and they fell in walking behind Ian and Vange.

Holding hands seemed much more intimate with Dall than it ever had before.

He readjusted their hands every so often so that their palms rubbed against each other.

This sent chills up her arm, even in the late May heat.

Once again, Emily was vaguely aware of the faire

atmosphere as the eight of them walked: mongers yelling "Hot cross buns." while throwing buns across the street to each other, women trying to wash their clothes on the rocks of a little stream but being heckled by ... pilgrims, people throwing rotten tomatoes at and saying funny curses at a Spaniard.

But as before, the faire was just background for the thrills going through her at the way Dall was holding her hand and how he hadn't wanted to part since they met.

Did we really just meet an hour ago?

She was even more thrilled by the attention Dall paid her.

As if they were old friends, he met her eye and shared everything with her. They laughed together when a peasant woman dragged her drunken husband through the faire by his nose—theatrically, of course. Emily could see she was really dragging him by the arm which held her hand on his nose.

Dall continued to make small talk, too.

"You did a good job choosing your clothes, you and the other lass."

"Thank you. It's nice of you to say so."

"Tis true, lass. You chose the authentic booth, so you can go wherever I go."

They smiled at each other intensely for a giddy moment.

But then he added something in a hurry.

"Wherever I go at the faire, I mean."

Slightly puzzled by that addition, but overly conscious that this gorgeous man was trying hard to put her at ease while she was letting him take all the burden of carrying the conversation, she scolded herself.

Wake up, Emily. Show some personality, or Dall is going to get bored of you.

But all she could think of to say was something really nerdy.

"Is Short Shakespeare one of those acting companies that do 'Romeo and Juliet' in twenty minutes, and then in fast forward, and then backwards?"

Oddly, Dall looked to Ian to answer her question.

It is opening day, but I would have sworn this wasn't Dall's first faire.

Ian got so excited that he forgot to use his Scottish accent and threw both his arms up in the air.

"Yeah, and they're really good."

Making one of her goofy faces, Vange teased Ian about dropping his accent. She mimicked him, throwing her own arms up.

"Oh, really?"

Everyone laughed.

Ian threw his arm back around Vange, and they all continued walking through the imitation English village, being solicited both by fake mongers and by people trying to get them to shop at all the booths that lined the street.

"Delicious and un-nutritious. Try the Queen's buns."

"We bet you five pounds you cannot climb this rope ladder."

"Chocolate. Iced. Cream."

One costumed group was more serious. There were a few dozen of them, all in raw homespun linen robes with garlands of flowers on top of their heads like hats, both men and women. Their area was a clump of standing stones visible off in the distance. They were all chanting, holding hands, and moving around the stones in a circle.

Emily wondered if the stones were real or just Styrofoam. It was hard to tell, this far away.

"Who are they?"

Dall answered without asking anyone.

"Those are druids."

Emily watched the druids circle around the stones until one of the building facades blocked her view. Just before it did, she noticed the guy with the dog tattoo watching her from the archery range, and then the facade blocked him, too.

janestain.com

67301219R00146

Made in the USA
Charleston, SC
11 February 2017